DEATH BY TOILET PAPER

"Ben is a character kids will root for, and he's surrounded by family and friends who help him see things will be okay, a message that may comfort readers facing similar circumstances." —*Publishers Weekly*

"Gephart's generous view of humanity's basic goodness shines through, and she leavens her characters' difficult situation with plenty of humor. . . . Readers can't help but enjoy this heartening book about hanging in there." —*Kirkus Reviews*

"Ben is a determined, likable character whom readers will doggedly root for, and Gephart infuses his story with humor and heart as she tenderly explores issues of grief, loss, family, and friendship." —*School Library Journal*

"[Gephart] again shows a deft hand at rendering difficult situations with empathy, adding just the right amount of realistic humor to relieve but not trivialize." —*The Bulletin*

ALSO BY DONNA GEPHART

*As If Being 12¾ Isn't Bad Enough,
My Mother Is Running for President!*

How to Survive Middle School

Olivia Bean, Trivia Queen

DEATH by TOILET PAPER

DONNA GEPHART

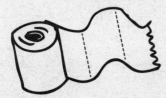

A YEARLING BOOK

Text copyright © 2014 by Donna Gephart
Cover art copyright © 2014 by David Coulson

All rights reserved. Published in the United States by Yearling, an imprint of Random House Children's Books, a division of Penguin Random House LLC, New York. Originally published in hardcover in the United States by Delacorte Press, an imprint of Random House Children's Books, New York, in 2014.

Yearling and the jumping horse design are registered trademarks of Penguin Random House LLC.

randomhousekids.com

Educators and librarians, for a variety of teaching tools, visit us at RHTeachersLibrarians.com

The Library of Congress has cataloged the hardcover edition of this work as follows:
Gephart, Donna.
Death by toilet paper / Donna Gephart. — First edition.
pages cm
Summary: Contest-crazed twelve-year-old Ben uses his wits and way with words in hopes of winning a prize that will keep his family from being evicted until his mother can pass her final CPA examination.
ISBN 978-0-385-74399-0 (hc) — ISBN 978-0-385-37416-3 (ebook) —
ISBN 978-0-375-99143-1 (glb)
[1. Contests—Fiction. 2. Moneymaking projects—Fiction. 3. Single-parent families—Fiction. 4. Toilet paper—Fiction.]
I. Title.
PZ7.G293463De 2014
[Fic]—dc23
2013026319

ISBN 978-0-385-37417-0 (pbk.)

Printed in the United States of America
10 9 8 7 6 5 4 3 2 1
First Yearling Edition 2015

TO MY SISTER ELLEN (AKA BATMAN).
Your determination and persistence inspire me,
and they inspired me to write this book.
Thank you for being there always and in all ways.

Dear Royal-T Toilet Paper Company,

You guys make the best toilet paper on the planet. I realize that's a weird thing for a seventh grader to say, but it's true. I didn't know enough to appreciate having Royal-T in our bathroom until the day it was gone—replaced by the world's worst recycled, scratchy (sand)paper.

Good toilet paper was the first thing to go; then cable got turned off, and it's gotten worse from there. Much worse.

But I don't feel like talking about that now.

I just want to tell you Royal-T is the best, and I wish we could go back to using it.

Your friend,
Benjamin Epstein

Seven percent of Americans steal toilet paper from hotel and motel rooms.

Inside my best friend's kitchen, blood spatters cover every surface—the kitchen table, including the pepper mill, the wall behind the table and much of the tile floor. Even their cat, Psycho, has a blood spatter across her white fur.

My eyes, open wide with horror, take in each gruesome detail.

Lying on the blood-spattered floor with a cleaver buried in his chest is my best friend's dad, Mr. Taylor. He's wearing his chef's apron from Chez Gourmet, but the apron is more red than white.

A trickle of blood leaks from the side of his mouth and drips into his beard, then onto the sticky floor. Mr. Taylor's right eyelid springs open.

He looks at me.

I step back, but his thick, hairy arm shoots out. He grabs my ankle, and his fingers squeeze with surprising strength. "Help . . . ," he gurgles. "Help me."

My voice explodes eight octaves too high, and I scream like a girl.

Toothpick lowers his video camera. "Cut! Great scream, Ben! Thanks, Dad." He does an awkward dance step that makes him look like an ostrich whose feet are on fire. "This is going to be my scariest film yet!"

Mr. Taylor (aka the corpse) leaps off the kitchen floor, removes the fake cleaver from his chest and pulls the bloody apron over his head. "You'd better get my apron clean before I leave for my shift at the restaurant tonight," he tells Toothpick, "or you're going to end up in there." Mr. Taylor points to a pot on the stove, where tomato sauce and severed fingers are bubbling.

Toothpick pulls the fake fingers out with tongs and tosses them into the sink. "Don't worry, Dad," he says. "Most of the fake blood is actually salsa. Looks great on film, and super easy to clean up."

"Tastes good, too," Mr. Taylor says, swiping his finger across the "blood" on the kitchen table and putting it in his mouth. "Needs a little cilantro, though."

Toothpick cracks up, and I get a pang in my chest, because I know my dad would have done something dumb like that, too. He was always doing silly things and cracking jokes, like "How do you get a baby astronaut to sleep? You rocket." When Mom and I didn't laugh, he'd say, "Rocket, rock it. Get it? Funny, right?"

I never imagined I'd miss my dad's dumb jokes.

"Now, get this salsa cleaned up," Mr. Taylor says, patting Toothpick's shoulder, "or I'm going to have to buy a truckload of nacho chips to go with it."

"No problemo," Toothpick says, slinging his skinny arm across my shoulders. He's more than a head taller than me, even though we're both twelve.

"Ben's going to help me clean everything," Toothpick says. "Right, buddy?"

"You know it," I say.

I don't mind helping Toothpick, because he pays me in the only currency a serious sweepstakes guy needs—stamps and, occasionally, postcards, envelopes and index cards—for all the good contests you can't enter online. And he lets me use his computer for the online sweeps. I don't like spending a stamp for each entry I mail in, but as serious sweepers on the message boards say, you've got to pay to play.

Helping Toothpick create his horror films is fun, especially when he lets me write the scripts. Not that there's much dialogue, other than a couple well-timed screams.

Guess Who We're Having for Dinner is the third, and I think the best, horror film he's made. The others were *The Terror Train Rides Again,* which we shot at 30th Street Station, and *Evil Penguins Take Over Philadelphia.* That one was hard to shoot, because we needed footage from the Philadelphia Zoo and the security guard kept yelling at us to quit leaning into the penguin enclosure. But it was the only way we were going to get the shot. When Toothpick almost fell in and I had to hoist him up by the back of his pants—which wasn't easy, especially with him screaming that his camera was going to fall in and get wet—we were escorted out of the zoo for "horsing around" and "making a ruckus."

Toothpick didn't mind, because his camera didn't fall in and he got the shot he wanted.

I minded, because it was embarrassing to be forced out of the zoo by the security guard. It reminded me of Dad, who used to work as a security guard at the *Inquirer* newspaper. Somehow, I felt like I'd disappointed him.

"Hey, Ben," Mr. Taylor says, wiping "blood" out of his beard with a paper towel. "There's an extra pan of lasagna in the fridge. Make sure you take it when you go. We're not going to eat it."

If Toothpick's mom still lived with them, she'd probably offer me some banana bread, too. She was always baking something delicious, and their house smelled so good when I visited.

"But, Dad," Toothpick whines, "I thought you said the lasagna—"

Mr. Taylor shoots a hard look at Toothpick, which silences him and tells me two things: That's not an *extra* pan of lasagna in their fridge. And no matter how hungry I am, that lasagna is staying right where it is. "Thanks, Mr. Taylor. We appreciate it."

"Anything for you and your mom," he says. "Hey, I'm going to take a snooze before work, so keep it down, all right?"

"Sure," I say.

"Psycho!" Toothpick screams, and he awkwardly lunges for his salsa-spattered cat so he can clean her fur. She leaps easily out of his grip and yowls.

"So much for quiet," Mr. Taylor says, shaking his head and walking upstairs.

Since Toothpick is chasing the cat with a wet paper towel and I don't feel like cleaning the entire kitchen by myself, I duck into their downstairs bathroom. Sitting on the toilet seat lid with my head in my hands, I wish Mr. Taylor hadn't offered me that lasagna. I'm sure it would taste great—everything he cooks does—but we don't need a handout. It makes me think of last week when our neighbor from across the hall, Mrs. Schneckle, stopped over with a bag of groceries from the market. She said she accidentally bought too much. No one *accidentally* buys too many groceries.

Things will get better, I tell myself, *because I will make them better.*

I promised.

Toothpick bangs on the bathroom door, which makes

my heart speed up. "Hey," he shouts. "You in there? You promised you'd help."

For a second, I think he's talking about helping my mom, and I feel a weight settle onto my heart like a stone. "Be right out," I manage. Then I count to six and flush so it sounds like I was really using the toilet the whole time.

My eyes are leaking a little, so I grab a few sheets of toilet paper to wipe them. The toilet paper is soft and fluffy, unlike the recycled junk Mom buys now. That stuff's so rough, I'd be better off wiping my butt with tree bark.

Before I realize what I'm doing, I pull off a long stretch, fold it and stuff it into the pocket of my jeans.

Back in the slightly less "bloody" kitchen, I feel like Toothpick has X-ray vision and can see the toilet paper inside my pocket.

Hoping to divert his attention, I ask, "What should I clean?"

"Psycho." Toothpick slaps a wet paper towel into my palm. "She's hiding behind the bookshelf in my room—getting salsa on everything—and I can't reach her."

"How am I going to?"

Toothpick puts a broom in my other hand.

"Funtastic," I say, making a mental note that "FUN-tastic" may be a good word combination for a future contest entry.

I hope that when I get Psycho out to clean her fur, she

doesn't use my arm as a scratching post, like she did once before. Then again, I've faced harder things.

Grasping my tools of terror—a broom handle and a wet paper towel—I charge into Toothpick's bedroom and issue a battle cry: "Yee-haaaaah!"

"Quiet!" Toothpick's dad bellows from his bedroom.

"Sorry, Mr. Taylor."

Downstairs, Toothpick laughs like a maniac.

FUNtastic!

That's how I spend my Saturday afternoon: doing fierce battle with a skittish, salsa-spattered cat, cleaning up after a bloody murder scene and taking toilet paper from my best friend's bathroom.

And *not* taking the lasagna from the Taylors' fridge.

Even though just thinking about it makes my mouth water like Niagara Falls.

Dear Benjamin Epstein,

Thank you for your letter. We appreciate your loyal-T to Royal-T Bathroom Tissue.

We, too, believe it's the best brand of bathroom tissue on the market today.

You might be interested to know that Royal-T Bathroom Tissue is sponsoring a contest to find a new slogan. (Details enclosed.)

Also enclosed, please find a coupon for a complimentary four-pack of Royal-T Bathroom Tissue.

Regards,
Ed Chase
Community Relations Representative,
   Royal-T Bathroom Tissue Company

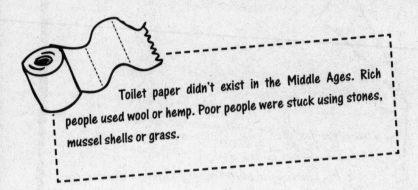

Toilet paper didn't exist in the Middle Ages. Rich people used wool or hemp. Poor people were stuck using stones, mussel shells or grass.

On the way home from school Monday, I spot our landlord, Mr. Katz, walking on the opposite side of the street.

I wave, but he must not see me, because he doesn't wave back.

Mom told me Mr. Katz and his business partner own four apartment buildings on our side of the street. Each building is exactly the same: three floors, with two apartments on each floor, plus a basement for laundry and storage. We pay $1,200 a month for our two-bedroom apartment. If everyone pays the same as we do, that's $28,800 a month for Mr. Katz and his partner.

Twenty-eight thousand eight hundred a month!

I shift my backpack and decide that when I grow up, I'm going to own a bunch of apartments. Then all I'll have to do is collect rent each month and fix things when they break.

And if my tenants can't pay on time, I'll be a nice guy and let them slide for a while.

I kick an empty WaWa coffee cup off the curb, wishing I had Mr. Katz's income for one month. Or even one week! That would solve all our problems.

Except one.

• • •

Inside the small foyer of our apartment building, I drop my backpack and pull the mailbox key from my pocket. There are six slim metal mailboxes along the wall, and ours is on the far left. It still says TODD EPSTEIN on the little window of the mailbox. I touch the plastic covering over Dad's name, wondering if Mom and I should replace it.

Nah. I'm glad it's still there.

Dad's voice was our answering machine message, too: "You've reached the Epsteins. We're too busy having fun to answer the phone right now, or we're ignoring you. Either way, leave us a message after the ..." I used to call our phone from Toothpick's house sometimes, just to hear Dad's voice. But when Mom couldn't pay the phone bill a few months ago, Dad's voice disappeared, along with phone service. Losing Dad nine months ago was the worst, and each time we lose something else—like phone service—it's a painful reminder.

I shake my head, dislodging those thoughts, and pull open the mailbox door, hoping it's not empty inside.

It's not!

One envelope is addressed to Mr. Benjamin Epstein, and it's from the Royal-T Bathroom Tissue Company. I rip the envelope open and find a letter inside, a coupon for a four-pack of free toilet paper and details about a new slogan contest. I'm surprised the contest wasn't listed in my *Sweeps-a-Lot* newsletter. "All right!" *My correspondence with Royal-T is paying off. The free toilet paper coupon and the contest information are definitely worth the stamp I used to mail them the letter.*

The other envelope is addressed to Shelley B. Epstein. Mom's name is Shelley Iris Epstein. I use Shelley B. Epstein (the "B" stands for Benjamin) for sweepstakes entries. I'm too young to enter most contests, so I use Mom's name, which is totally legal. Lots of sweepers use other people's names or variations of their own names. It's common practice. But if I win a big prize, it will be under Mom's name, not mine. And her picture will probably appear in *Sweeps-a-Lot*. I wouldn't like that, but it would still be cool to win something big.

What's in this envelope could be BIG!

It's from the convenience store WaWa, which means I might have won the grand prize in their Name-a-Sandwich

Sweepstakes: a new car! I thought my entry was good but didn't realize it was *this* good.

I press the envelope to my chest, hoping for my first grand-prize win. *Mom will flip if we win a car.* No more walking or taking buses everywhere. Or we could sell the car for piles of cash.

Mrs. Schneckle walks downstairs with a basket of laundry balanced on her hip. She pushes her short silvery hair to one side. "Something good in the mail today, *bubeleh*?"

"I don't know yet," I say. But in my pounding heart, I know it's something amazing.

Mrs. Schneckle puts her basket down with a thump and waits. "I had only junk mail today," she says. "And yesterday. And the day before that. *Pfft!*"

With shaking hands, I slide my finger under the WaWa envelope flap. I reach in and pull out . . . a coupon for a free WaWa hoagie.

My shoulders slump.

"Nu?" Mrs. Schneckle asks. "What did you win?"

Not a grand prize. I hold up the coupon. "A free WaWa hoagie." I swallow hard. "They gave out a hundred of these prizes."

"Congratulations," she says. "They give me gas. But they're delicious."

I grab Mrs. Schneckle's laundry basket and carry it downstairs for her. She follows me to the basement, which smells like mold and laundry soap.

Maybe I should stop hoping for a grand-prize win.

Maybe I should stop entering sweepstakes. But there's the new Royal-T Bathroom Tissue slogan contest. If I win that grand prize, it will change everything for Mom and me.

"I also got a coupon for four free rolls of Royal-T," I say, dropping Mrs. Schneckle's basket on top of the washing machine.

"That's the brand I use," she says. "Good stuff."

I feel a pang because we can't afford it anymore. But at least now we'll have four free rolls.

"Great job, *bubeleh*." Mrs. Schneckle squeezes my shoulder and starts the washer. "Did you have to write anything clever to win those prizes?"

Mrs. Schneckle has lived across the hall from us forever, so she knows I'm the Sultan of Sweepstakes. The King of Contests. The Guru of Giveaways. The Wizard of Winning.

Mom tells her every time I snag a good prize, like when I won a year's supply of Boaty Oats Instant Oatmeal for coming up with a fun new way to eat their oatmeal. I suggested crumbling an Oreo cookie into it and adding brown sugar and cinnamon on top. Toothpick's dad helped me with that part.

I'd hoped to win their grand prize—twenty-five hundred dollars and a trip to New York City for two people—but I won first prize instead, which was enough boxes of plain instant oatmeal to give a bunch to Mrs. Schneckle and to Zeyde Jake—my grandfather—and still have enough to last us a year.

Too bad I hate plain oatmeal. And Oreo cookies and brown sugar are not in our budget at this time.

Mom also told Mrs. Schneckle when I won the barbecue grill for coming up with the slogan "Thrillin' to Be Chillin' and Grillin' with My Genie's Genius Barbecue Grill." Again, I'd hoped for the grand prize of five thousand dollars but got the first prize of a brand-new Genie's Genius Grill, which is still in its box in my bedroom closet, along with T-shirts, baseball caps, a cookbook and beach towels I've won over the years.

"Yes," I tell Mrs. Schneckle as she adds liquid soap to the washer, "my entry for the WaWa contest was 'My Piled-High, Mile-High, Please-Pass-the-Pie Sandwich.'"

"Clever," Mrs. Schneckle says, poking my head with her finger. "You've got a big brain in there, Benjamin. How do you keep track of all these contests?"

I shrug. "I write down each contest I enter and whether it was mail-in or online. Then, when I read about who won on the sweepers online message board, I cross it off my list. I have about thirty entries out to different contests right now."

"That's fantastic," she says.

Her compliment makes me feel good. "My aunt Abby used to sweep. She got me into the hobby a few years ago, but she doesn't do it anymore." I turn to go. "Well, I've got to work on my entry for Royal-T's new contest. I'm going to win the grand prize this time, Mrs. Schneckle."

On my way upstairs, she calls, "When you win, don't forget the little people!"

I laugh as I let myself into our apartment, because Mrs. Schneckle is little. Even though I'm one of the shortest guys in seventh grade, I'm still taller than she is.

In our apartment, I throw my backpack on the couch, spread my sweepstakes supplies on the kitchen table—paper, pencils, envelopes and stamps—and realize something's missing. If I hope to create a grand-prize-worthy slogan, I'll need inspiration . . . in the form of toilet paper.

I go to the shelf in the bathroom and pull out all the rolls of lousy gray toilet paper we have and pile them in the center of the kitchen table, wishing I'd saved the good toilet paper from Toothpick's house the other day. But I used it as soon as I got home.

I grab a roll of the gray, scratchy stuff and write, "Be the best you can be with Royal-T." *Lame!* I rearrange the rolls into a pyramid, stare at it and write, "Royal-T is tops—way better than using a tree." *Terrible!*

How am I going to come up with a brilliant slogan when I'm hungry? The school lunch lasts only so long.

I lay my head on my hands and prepare to wallow in frustration when the front door opens.

"Mom!"

I hope she brought something good to eat, even though lately it's been nothing but the All-Pancake Channel when she comes home.

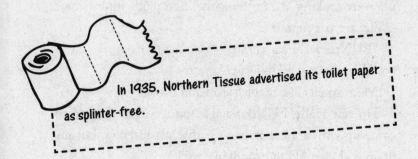

In 1935, Northern Tissue advertised its toilet paper as splinter-free.

"How's my favorite son?" Mom asks, dropping a take-out box in front of me.

I push it off my paper, knowing exactly what's inside from the smell. "I'm your only son," I remind her. "And I'm doing FUNtastic." *Use Royal-T. It's FUNtastic.*

Ugh!

"I'm working on a slogan for Royal-T," I say, pointing to the toilet paper; then I tap my head to remind Mom to take off her paper piggy hat.

"Oh!" Mom says, pulling out clips and grabbing the Piggy's Pancake House hat off her head. "I can't believe I left this idiotic thing on while I was studying at the library."

Mom jams the hat into her back pocket. "No wonder people were looking at me strangely." She plops into a chair. "Why are you fantastic?"

"FUNtastic," I correct.

"Why are you FUNtastic?"

Mom smells like maple syrup and bacon.

I'm not really FUNtastic. I'm hungry, and I need to come up with a great slogan for this sweepstakes, but my brain is sludge. "How'd studying go?"

Mom leans back. "Well, financial accounting and reporting are not exactly exciting topics." Mom yawns, as if to prove her point. "But I kept at it, because I have to ace the big test." She gives me a playful punch in the shoulder. "Right?"

"Absolutely," I say. Mom has to pass the fourth CPA exam to get her license. Then she'll land a great job as an accountant instead of working at Piggy's Pancake House. It's all part of Dad's Grand Plan.

Dad came up with the Grand Plan before he got sick. He stuck it to the fridge with our HAVING FUN IN FLORIDA magnet and said, "This document is like the Constitution. It can be amended, but the core principles must remain intact."

Since then, Mom has made exactly one amendment to the Grand Plan.

GRAND PLAN
1. Dad will work extra hours so Mom can study for

and take the four CPA (Certified Public Accoun-
tant) exams.

2. *Mom will pass all four exams with flying colors*
   and receive her CPA license.

3. *With her license and work experience, Mom will*
   get a GREAT job as a CPA.

4. *Dad will then be able to work fewer hours, so*
   he can spend more time at home, painting and
   hanging out with his favorite son, Benjamin.

Result: Mom and Ben will have a better life.

The Grand Plan has been hanging on our fridge a long time, but I still glance at it every day, and it still motivates Mom and me to do what we need to.

Mom leans over and kisses the top of my head, which probably stinks because we had to run a mile in PE today and I haven't showered since. There's no way I'm ever going to shower after PE with Angus Andrews in my class. He'd probably steal my clothes and drop them in the toilet or throw them out the window. I don't know why they mix eighth graders with seventh graders in PE.

Angus already has stubble, a deep voice, stinky armpits and enough underarm hair to braid.

So far, I have only the stinky-armpits part. But it's not too bad.

Mom grabs my paper and reads my lousy Royal-T slogans out loud. "New contest?" she asks.

I show her the sweepstakes information from Royal-T.

"Whoa, Benjamin! Ten thousand dollars? That's a doozy!"

"I can win it," I say.

"I have no doubt."

"And I got more mail today." I hand Mom the coupon for the free four-pack of toilet paper.

"Oooh," she says. "I'll pick it up next time I'm at the ACME."

I love seeing Mom so happy over something so small. I'd never thought about it, but maybe she's as disappointed as I am that we had to switch to the cheap stuff. I reach into my pocket. "Can you use this?" I hand her the WaWa hoagie coupon, even though I was hoping to split a fat hoagie with Toothpick this weekend, to make up for all the food he shares with me at lunch.

Mom wraps my fingers around the coupon. "No, Ben. You keep this. I'm sure you earned it." Then she taps the take-out box with her fingernail. "Brought you home pancakes."

"Really? I'd never have guessed."

"These are different. Pumpkin pecan. A special flavor for fall."

I open the box, take a nibble and close it.

"You must be sick of me bringing home pancakes," Mom says, whisking the box off the table. "They're coming out of our ears. Let's see what else we have."

On my paper, I draw a pancake coming out of an ear.

It looks like a Frisbee in a dog's mouth. That's why I enter contests that require a way with words, not art. You'd think I'd be good at art, since Dad was—Mom has a bunch of his paintings in her bedroom closet—but I guess I didn't inherit his artistic gene.

Mom returns to the table with crackers covered with thin slices of American cheese. We've had that coming out of our ears, too, but I don't say anything.

I grab a few crackers and chow down, pretending they're hot, gooey slices of Kirk's Pizza—my favorite kind. Unfortunately, when it comes to pretending food is something it isn't, my imagination is weak.

And my imagination is apparently weak when it comes to creating grand-prize-winning ideas, too. *Royal-T, from the finest tree, makes you clean and happy.* Awful. *Use Royal-T and you'll see it's the best there can be.* Hopeless.

As punishment for my lousy ideas and in hopes of jogging loose better ones, I bonk myself in the head with a roll of our gray, scratchy toilet paper, probably giving myself abrasions from splinters!

"Who's winning?" Mom asks, cracker crumbs flying from her mouth. "You or the toilet paper?"

"Not me," I say, putting down the roll. "I can't come up with anything good."

"Let me read the requirements," Mom says.

Royal-T Bathroom Tissue is looking for a new slogan. In twenty-five words or fewer,

**tell people why Royal-T is the softest,
strongest bathroom tissue available today.
Grand prize: $10,000**

"That's at least four hundred dollars a word," Mom says.

"Spoken like a true accountant." I shove a cracker into my mouth and swallow hard. "Did you register for the exam yet?"

"This morning," Mom says. "And it wasn't easy to fork over the ninety-five-dollar fee. Then when I get my confirmation packet, I'll still have to pay one ninety thirty-five to sign up for the actual test."

"I know it's expensive, Mom, but . . ."

She reaches across the table and touches my hand. "It's part of the Grand Plan."

I glance at Dad's empty kitchen chair and feel tightness in my chest.

"Don't worry, Benjamin." At first I think Mom's talking about Dad's empty chair, but then she says, "I have the money saved specifically for that last test."

My shoulders relax. "That's good."

"But what's not good is this." She reaches into her pocket and pulls out a stack of ones. "Thirty-seven dollars in tips today."

That sounds like a lot of money to me.

"And let's not forget this bonanza." She reaches into her pocket and pulls out two quarters. "Some jokers left my tip in a puddle of syrup. I had to wash the quarters off in the bathroom."

I press my lips together, hating the thought of my mom picking out those sticky quarters.

She presses the heel of her hand into her forehead. "Mr. Katz gave me extra time to pay the rent again this month. But I'm still behind from last month and ..." She taps the pile of ones. "So we owe most of August's rent and all twelve hundred from September's. I can't believe how quickly we went through the savings, and Dad's medical bills were ..." Mom inhales sharply. "I don't know how long Mr. Katz will be able to let us slide." She spreads her money on the table. "And I'll need a lot more of these if—"

Someone knocks on our door.

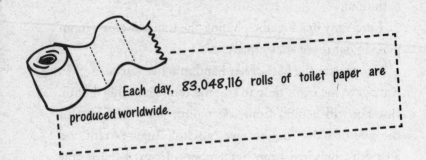

Each day, 83,048,116 rolls of toilet paper are produced worldwide.

A deep worry wrinkle forms between Mom's eyebrows. She smoothes her unsmoothable curly hair, walks to the door and opens it a few inches. "Hello, Mr. Katz."

"Shelley," Mr. Katz says.

I can't see him, but I picture Mr. Katz's thin lips and bushy eyebrows. He should mow those things.

"It's time to pay the rent," he says. "Actually, it's well past time."

At the table, I keep working on my slogan. I'm determined to win the grand prize this time. "Royal-T is good for your posterior. For your rear-e-or. Your—"

"Give me a second, Mr. Katz. I'll go get it."

Mom grabs the thirty-seven dollars off the kitchen table, then I follow her to her bedroom.

Even though her back is to me, I see Mom take two envelopes from her bureau drawer. Not just the rent envelope but another one, too.

"No," I say, and grab the envelope marked GRAND PLAN.

"Just this one time, Ben." Mom touches my cheek. "To help pay the rent. I'm sure we'll be able to build it up again." And she snatches the GRAND PLAN envelope from me.

"Mom, you need that money to take the last test!"

The worry wrinkle between Mom's eyebrows deepens. "I know, but—"

"Hello?" Mr. Katz calls.

"Be right there!" Mom leans down and whispers, "Benjamin, I have to."

The framed wedding photo of Mom and Dad over the bureau catches my attention. I feel like Dad's looking at me, expecting me to do something.

I grab Mom's hand. "Please!"

Gripping the envelopes as though her life depends on them, Mom glances at the wedding photo, then drops the GRAND PLAN envelope back into her drawer.

A weight drops off my heart.

I follow Mom to the door, but she nudges me back toward the table, on the other side of our living room/ dining room/kitchen.

I pretend to write but am straining to hear their conversation.

"We're still short," Mom says.

"How short?" Mr. Katz asks.

If Dad were alive, he'd have said something smart-alecky, like "Oh, about four feet." Actually, if Dad were alive, we'd have paid our rent on time, because he would probably still be working at the *Inquirer*.

Mom's quiet. I know she's thinking of the $190.35 exam money in her bureau drawer. "We still owe you eighteen hundred dollars."

My heart pounds.

"Look, Shelley," Mr. Katz says. "I know what you've been through. If it were up to me, I'd let you slide a while longer, but my business partner won't allow any more extensions. I'm sorry."

I press my pencil so hard it pokes a hole through the paper.

"You've been more than generous," Mom says. "But work's been slow lately. I'll need a little more time. Another small grace period."

The worried sound in Mom's voice knots my stomach into a pretzel, but not the good, soft kind served warm with salt and spicy mustard.

"Shelley, I hate to say this, but there are plenty of other people who would jump at a chance to rent this place."

A door creaks open, and Mrs. Schneckle's voice erupts from the hallway. "Show me one person eager to rent that apartment! This place isn't exactly the Palace of Versailles, you know. You're lucky to have Shelley. She and Ben are great tenants!"

Go, Mrs. Schneckle!

"Hello, Mrs. Schneckle," Mr. Katz says, as though he's totally worn out. *Maybe being a landlord isn't the easiest job after all.* "I've got no problem with you. You always pay your rent on time. Please go back into your apartment."

My stomach knots into a hundred pretzels. *Mom works hard and would pay the rent on time if she could. She's trying!*

"Ah, give her a break," Mrs. Schneckle says. "Be a *mensch.*"

There's a pause, then I hear Mrs. Schneckle's apartment door slam.

"Okay, Shelley," Mr. Katz says. "But this is the last time I'll be able to do this for you. I'll be back this Friday, the twenty-fifth—in four days. If you don't have the rest of the rent—the entire amount—I'm going to have to file eviction papers. I'm sorry, but my hands are tied."

I get up and quietly walk to a spot a few steps behind Mom. I don't want her to feel like she's alone.

"But . . . ," Mom says.

Her tiny word hangs in the air, a speck—a molecule—next to the giant word sucking all the air out of the apartment building: "EVICTION."

"I'll try to get the money," Mom says in a flat tone. "Thank you, Mr. Katz. I appreciate it."

I reach for Mom's elbow, pull Mom inside and close the door.

Her eyes are wide and glassy. She looks dazed, like she did the day we came home from Dad's funeral.

"You did it," I say quietly. "You got us another extension. That's good. Right?"

Mom leans against the door and closes her eyelids. "Oh, Benjamin," she whispers. "Even if I could get enough money by Friday"—she opens her eyelids—"which I can't . . . only a week later October's rent will be due. Another twelve hundred." Mom lets out a ragged breath, walks to the kitchen table and sinks onto her chair. Gazing up at the ceiling, she asks, "How am I supposed to do this?"

I know who she's asking, and it isn't me.

I look at Dad's recliner in the living room/dining room/kitchen—the one where he watched all the Eagles football games and screamed at the refs. I focus on the carpet in front of the couch, where we used to wrestle like maniacs until Mom made us stop. I think of the mural he painted and the glow-in-the-dark stars on my bedroom ceiling.

Almost every memory I have of Dad is in this apartment. We can't leave.

I bend over my paper with the pencil-point puncture in it. "Royal-T is good for your posterior," I write. "It's super soft on your rear-e-or." *Good.*

"Ben?"

"Pamper your posterior." *Excellent.*

"Ben!"

I look up.

Mom's worry wrinkle is the deepest I've ever seen it. "I'm going to have to spend the CPA exam money," she says. "I wish I hadn't sent in the ninety-five dollars to register. I wish—"

"Mom, Mr. Daniels is your best customer at the diner. He said you've got a great work ethic and mad math skills. Remember when you fixed the check his waitress messed up and he asked you about your background?"

Mom nods.

"And when you told him about how close you were to becoming a certified public accountant and about your last job, he promised you a job at his accounting firm?"

Mom bites her bottom lip and nods again.

"Just as soon as you pass the fourth test and get your license." I don't say *a job where you won't have to wear that stupid paper pig hat.* "A good accounting job!"

"I know, Ben, and I really want that. But we won't have enough time. I need eighteen hundred dollars by Friday. Honey, you know I make only about five hundred a week with salary and tips." Mom presses the heel of her hand into her forehead. "How did we burn through the savings so fast?"

"Dad's medical bills," I mutter.

"Oh, there were all kinds of bills," Mom says. "Hey, at least I'll get the social security check for you at the beginning of October. That'll be another six hundred. Unfortunately, it won't come in time to pay Mr. Katz this Friday."

Mom sinks even lower in her chair. "I don't know what we're going to do, Benjamin."

"We'll figure something out," I say, squeezing my pencil so hard I'm surprised it doesn't snap. *I'll figure something out.*

I take my paper and pencil and one roll of lousy toilet paper and walk down the hall toward my bedroom.

"Ben?"

I pretend I don't hear Mom.

"Benjamin?"

Without answering, I go into my room and shut the door.

But all the worry comes in with me.

I throw the paper, pencil and toilet paper on my desk. I can't think about the contest right now. Even if I wrote the best entry on the planet, I couldn't win the cash prize in time to pay the September rent and the rest of the August rent by this Friday.

Lying on my bed, I press a fist into my stomach because the crackers and cheese didn't make a dent in my hunger. I remember the time I won a hundred-dollar gift certificate to the supermarket for telling why I loved our neighborhood ACME store. I used Mom's name and wrote, "Our ACME puts the FUN in FUNctional!" While it was only a third-place winner, our fridge and pantry were stuffed with delicious food for a week. I wish I'd win something like that again.

To take my mind off the landlord's visit and our crummy situation, I open a big book called the *Bathroom Reader*. Dad had thought it was funny to keep it in our hallway bathroom. Now I keep it on the desk by my bed to read when I have trouble falling asleep. Unfortunately, the fun facts don't distract me now, so I hurl the book across the room. It hits the far wall with a satisfying crash and lands on the daybed Toothpick uses when he sleeps over.

"You okay?" Mom calls.

No! "Yes," I yell. "I'm superrific." Sometimes I'm also the Sultan of Sarcasm.

I lie on my back, staring at the galaxy Dad painted on my bedroom ceiling. Blue comets streaking across the nighttime sky, a golden crescent moon, bright red shooting stars and dozens of press-on, glow-in-the-dark stars. A few of the glow-in-the-dark stars have fallen off, but I've climbed on a chair and glued them back on. Luckily, the ceiling in my room is low, so I can reach it when I need to.

"Eighteen hundred dollars is so much money," I say to no one. "How are we going to get that much money by this Friday without spending the Grand Plan money? Not that the one ninety thirty-five we're saving to pay for Mom's final accounting exam is going to help much anyway."

I examine each part of Dad's galaxy, remembering how focused he looked while he was painting it. A chasm slightly larger than the universe opens in my chest. I think about the toilet-paper pyramid on our kitchen table made up of the world's worst toilet paper. I think about Mom counting out her lousy dollar bills and almost—almost—taking the Grand Plan money to pay the stupid rent and back rent.

I grab my pillow and hug it to my chest. The only thing I know for sure is I could never sleep anywhere except under Dad's galaxy.

I roll to my side and watch Barkley—my blue betta fish with the swishy royal-blue fins—swim around his tank like nothing has changed, like the landlord didn't just threaten to kick us out. Like everything on the planet is fine, thank you very much.

When I begged Mom and Dad for a dog a couple years ago, they said no. They said, "Not enough space." They said, "Not allowed in the apartment."

Dad came home after work the next day with a fish. "Closest I could come to a dog for you, pal. He'll keep you good company."

So I named the fish Barkley—the name I was saving for a dog—and he has kept me good company ever since. I'm careful to keep Barkley's water clean and feed him regularly so he'll live a long life. I know he's counting on me. Luckily, fish food is cheap, and Mom bought me a couple packages back when we had more money.

Only problem is that if Barkley were an actual dog— one made of warm fur and a wagging tail—he'd jump on my bed right now and lick my face and curl up next to me, so I could pet his silky ears and feel slightly less empty inside. And maybe if Dad were still alive, we'd have moved into a house by now and he'd have painted a new galaxy of shooting stars on my bedroom ceiling and I'd have gotten an actual dog and named him Fishy or something stupid like that.

I stare at the glow-in-the-dark stars and throw my pillow at Dad's galaxy. "Why'd you have to die?" I scream.

"Ben?" Mom calls.

"I'm okay!" I lie.

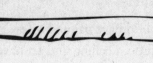

Dear Mr. Ed Chase,

It looks like we might get evicted from our apartment. Soon!

Does your company have any jobs a seventh grader can do? I get good grades in school—mostly—and I'm super good at writing and coming up with creative ideas. If you have an online job, I could do it from the library or my friend Toothpick's house. We used to have a computer, but last month Mom sold it to someone she works with because we needed the money.

Also, I like your toilet paper. A lot.

Thanks,
Benjamin Epstein

Toilet paper for the average person was invented by an American, Joseph Gayetty, in 1857 but didn't catch on for a while. In those days, housewives had to ask the grocer for every item they bought, and many were too embarrassed to ask for toilet paper.

In the Remington Middle School cafeteria, which smells like boiled hot dogs and cleaning solution, I get my free lunch—a hot dog on a bun, crinkle-cut French fries and peas and carrots, each in little compartments on a plastic tray—and take it to the table I share with Toothpick.

"Hey." Toothpick peels the top layer of bread off a mozzarella, tomato and basil sandwich. He picks off the basil and puts it on his napkin.

I take it and eat it.

"How can you eat that stuff?" Toothpick asks. "It's gross. And part of the napkin got stuck to it."

"Extra fiber," I say, and chew with exaggerated motion. Toothpick's lucky his dad is a chef. I wish someone made me fancy lunches every day so I didn't have to get free school lunches.

Toothpick hands me an apple and a Snickers bar—my favorite kind of candy—because his dad always packs him more food than he can eat.

"Thanks, Pick." I chomp into the juicy apple, remembering hearing that you get more energy from eating an apple than from drinking a cup of coffee. I hope it's true.

"Want to help edit *Guess Who We're Having for Dinner* after school?"

"Sure," I say, thinking that Pick will probably have awesome snacks at his house, "but I have to work on my contest entry for Royal-T toilet paper, too. Ten-thousand-dollar grand prize."

"Awesome." Toothpick gives me a fist bump.

"Hey," I say, wiping juice off my chin with the back of my hand. "Can you think of a way—"

"Hi, guys." Delaney Phillips drops a full box of Golly Pops onto our table. "Fifty cents each or four for a dollar. We're earning money for our band trip to Hershey."

Delaney says it like it's the nine-millionth time she's had to say the same thing. Zero enthusiasm. Of course, her lack of zeal could be because she's talking to Toothpick and me. Not too many girls at school get excited to talk to us, unless you count the tech teacher, Mrs. Gillespie. And she only gets excited to talk to Toothpick because he's president of her audiovisual club and helps her edit film projects.

"No thanks," Toothpick says, holding up a Twix bar. "We have better stuff."

Delaney makes a face, grabs her box and swivels to go.

"I'll buy four," I say, because sometimes my mouth works before my brain has a chance to hit the override switch. I don't want to give up my dollar. It's the last of ten bucks Aunt Abby sent me in a card when school started.

"Thanks, Ben," Delaney says, snatching the dollar from my fingers and flashing me a thousand-watt smile. She has blue rubber bands on her braces.

I realize a dollar can't buy much, but it just bought me a huge smile from Delaney. I pick out two watermelon and two grape Golly Pops and watch her walk to the next table.

Other kids reach into their pockets and hand her money.

Toothpick picks up his Twix bar, but before he rips open the wrapper, I get a sweet idea and snatch it from his skinny fingers.

"Hey! Give it back!"

"I need it," I say.

"You need it?" Toothpick says. "I need it. It's mine! I gave you the Snickers."

I feel Toothpick's stare on my back as I go to the next table, carrying his Twix bar and my Snickers bar.

"I'm selling candy bars," I say.

"How much?" someone asks.

"Buck apiece."

Before I know it, the candy bars in my hand are replaced by two dollar bills.

I return and slap the bills onto the table in front of Toothpick.

He grabs one of the bills and shoves it in his pocket. "You still owe me a Twix bar. I'm hungry."

I know Toothpick will get over being mad, and this is important. I've just come up with an idea that might save Mom and me from getting evicted. I shove the other dollar into my pocket.

"Pick?" I ask, sliding back onto my seat and taking a huge bite of hot dog. "How can I make fifty bucks really fast?" I ask, my mouth full.

"Rob a bank?"

"Legally."

"Hmm. What do you need the money for? More sweepstakes supplies?"

I don't want to tell him it's to help out Mom. "Um, yeah," I say, as though it's no big deal. "So . . . any great ideas?"

"Sell your spleen."

"Might need that," I say, poking my side, wondering where my spleen actually is and what it does. "Any less painful ideas?"

Toothpick unwraps one of the grape Golly Pops. "Sell something else," he says. "What do you have? I mean, besides acne and bad breath?"

I kick him under the table. I have just a few zits, and the one time I know I had bad breath was when Mom "forgot" to buy toothpaste, but that happened only once.

"Got it!" I say a little too loudly, because a few kids at the end of our table turn to look at me. I lean across the table and whisper, "My barbecue grill. That's got to be worth at least fifty bucks. Right?"

"I guess." Toothpick shrugs.

"How will I sell it, though? It's not like anyone at school would want to buy a barbecue grill."

Pick points his mauled Golly Pop at me. "The Internet, my good man. I'll bet we have it sold before dinner."

Genius. I want to leap over the table and give Toothpick a huge hug, but no way I'm doing that in the middle of the cafeteria at Remington Middle School. I'd like to live to see eighth grade.

"Let's meet at my apartment after school." After finishing my hot dog and fries, I unwrap a Golly Pop. "We can edit your movie afterward. Sound good?"

Toothpick nods, and for the first time in a while, I feel fantastic, because I know that if this plan actually works— and it will!—I might have come up with the solution to our rent problem. Mom and I will be able to make it until she passes that last CPA exam and gets the accounting job at Mr. Daniels's firm.

I shove the watermelon Golly Pop in my mouth, knowing Dad would be proud of me.

In 1879, brothers Clarence and E. Ervin Scott founded the Scott Paper Company in Philadelphia and began successfully marketing toilet paper to the public.

4:25 p.m.: At the apartment, I touch Dad's name on our mailbox for luck, but our box contains only a dumb bill from the electric company.

4:45 p.m.: Toothpick has eaten two pancakes from a take-out container in the fridge, shot a photo of the barbecue grill with his smartphone and listed it on SellSpace, a free site where people buy and sell things locally.

5:10 p.m.: We receive our first email response from our ad. It's from a prince in Nigeria who wants us to send our bank account information. Delete!

5:21 p.m.: We receive our second email, from a guy offering to buy the grill for sixty dollars.

5:22 p.m.: Toothpick and I high-five each other, jump around the room and generally dork out.

5:24 p.m.: Toothpick replies where and when we'll meet the guy to sell him the grill.

5:25 p.m.: The guy agrees. And says he's bringing cash!

5:26 p.m.: Another brief dork-out moment.

5:29 p.m.: Toothpick and I carry the boxed barbecue grill four blocks to the WaWa parking lot. (Note: This is harder than it sounds, because the grill is heavy and the one who walks backward the whole way is me.)

5:48 p.m.: A guy pulls up in a white pickup truck. He has no trouble spotting us, because we're the only two people with a large boxed barbecue grill.

5:52 p.m.: The man seems surprised that we're just kids and asks where we got the grill. I don't think he believes I won it, but he puts two twenties and two tens in my hand and hoists the grill onto the back of his pickup truck and drives away, so I don't really care what he thinks.

6:01 p.m.: Toothpick and I go into WaWa (aka The World's Best Convenience Store). It's warm and bright and smells like coffee and fresh bread. I give Toothpick the free-hoagie coupon I won. It's my way of saying thanks for all his help. Then I use ten dollars from the guy and the dollar I earned from selling a candy bar at lunch to buy chips and Shorti Hoagies for Mom and me. I get banana peppers on hers, because she loves those gross little yellow things.

Then Toothpick and I pick out a hundred of the best candy bars WaWa sells, almost emptying their boxes near the cash register. The candy bars are on sale—two for one dollar—so it costs fifty bucks. I hate to hand over the money, but I know it's the only way to make my new business idea work. The clerk raises her eyebrows at all our candy bars, but she doesn't say anything.

6:26 p.m.: Toothpick heads off to his house, because his dad is making a risotto—whatever the heck that is. Pick says he'll eat the hoagie for dessert and thanks me.

6:27 p.m.: I lug home a hundred candy bars and the hoagies in two bags, which feels like weight lifting (but is not nearly as heavy as carrying a barbecue grill).

6:28 p.m.: I realize I never helped Toothpick edit his film, like I said I would.

6:29 p.m.: I vow to make it up to him, while trying to find a way to carry the bags so they don't feel so heavy.

6:42 p.m.: I make it home with what feels like two broken arms.

6:44 p.m.: In my room, I empty my backpack of three textbooks, a composition book and a loose-leaf binder, then fill the space with two WaWa bags full of candy bars. I imagine my backpack completely stuffed with dollar bills tomorrow and grin at Barkley. I know it's impossible, but it seems like he presses his fishy lips against the glass of his tank and grins back.

6:57 p.m.: Mom comes home from studying at the library. When she sees the WaWa Shorti Hoagies on our table, her smile is an even higher wattage than Delaney's was at lunch today.

6:59 p.m.: Mom notices I remembered banana peppers on her hoagie, and she kisses the top of my head. "Benjamin Epstein, you're the best. You must've spent all the money Aunt Abby sent you to buy these hoagies." I don't tell Mom where I really got the money, so technically I'm not lying. But in my heart, it feels like I am.

8:04 p.m.: Between the candy bars that fill my backpack and the delicious Shorti Hoagie and chips that satisfy my stomach, I feel pretty terrific. Even though I'm doing history homework. And it's boring.

9:16 p.m.: I can't concentrate on creating a winning slogan for the Royal-T Bathroom Tissue contest, because I'm so excited about selling candy bars tomorrow.

9:42 p.m.: Lying in bed, with only the dim light from the streetlamp outside and my stomach still feeling full, I say goodnight to Barkley, then stare up at the green glow-in-the-dark stars and tell Dad everything's going to be okay, that I've got it covered.

9:43 p.m.: I wish he could answer me.

9:44 p.m.: I wish he could answer me.

9:45 p.m.: I wish . . .

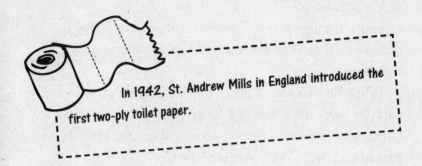

In 1942, St. Andrew Mills in England introduced the first two-ply toilet paper.

Selling candy bars during lunch is easy.

Kids can't hand me their dollar bills fast enough. Some kids buy two or three at a time. *Why didn't I think of doing this sooner?*

When lunch period ends, my backpack is stuffed not with candy bars but with a hundred dollar bills, just like I imagined!

I'll need to spend fifty dollars to buy more candy bars for tomorrow. That means I'll earn fifty dollars in profit every school day. That's an amazing amount of money, but it won't be enough to pay the eighteen hundred dollars due in two days! Maybe if we give Mr. Katz the money from my candy sales and Mom's tips and salary, he'll be able to let us slide a little longer.

I resist the urge to treat myself to an ice cream sandwich, because we'll need all the money I have. I can't waste any right now.

When I let Toothpick peek at the cash inside my backpack, he gives me a hard fist bump and half an almond-butter-and-strawberry-jam sandwich, because his dad packed him two. "That's awesome, Ben."

"Awesome," I agree, my mouth full.

"Way better than selling your spleen."

"Way better," I say.

We both crack up.

After school, I go to the Northeast Regional Library on Cottman Avenue to do my homework and look up information about evictions. I learn some interesting things about eviction law in Philadelphia, like how many days we really have to pay before we get thrown out. I don't learn anything interesting from doing my history homework, but I write long, funny sentences using our vocabulary words for Mrs. Durlofsky's language arts assignment. I know she'll love my creative sentences, some of which are over three lines long!

Then I go to WaWa and buy a hundred more candy bars.

This time, the guy who rings me up looks at me strangely as I pull fifty crumpled bills from my backpack. "You've got some sweet tooth there, kid!"

The lady behind me in line laughs. "Your dentist is going to love you."

Feeling my cheeks heat up, I nod, pay for the candy bars and hightail it out of there. Why I need to buy a hundred candy bars is nobody's business. Maybe I'll go to a different WaWa next time, even though it's farther away.

The cool air feels great on my warm cheeks as I walk home.

I figure if I eat a couple candy bars, the bag will get lighter, but I don't want to literally eat into my profits.

For some reason, the bags of candy bars don't feel as heavy as last time.

Maybe it's because I don't also have hoagies and chips in the bags, or maybe it's because I'm getting stronger.

At home, Barkley watches me stuff the bills into a paper bag and stuff it in the back of my underwear drawer. I love having so much money.

• • •

The next day, Thursday, I sell every candy bar before lunch is even over and have time to sit with Toothpick and share his fruit salad and mini blueberry muffins before the bell rings. They go well with my grilled cheese, fries and salad. I keep peeking into my backpack to look at all that lovely green, crumpled money.

After school, I go to the WaWa almost a mile farther away, but it's worth it, because the store's really crowded and no one says anything when I buy a hundred candy bars.

Friday is my best candy bar sales day ever. Word's gotten around, so people stop me in the hall between classes. By the time lunch is halfway over, I have only four left to sell.

I'm standing at Trevor Duxbury and Brice Reid's lunch table, hoping to unload my inventory and get back to Toothpick before he eats all his lunch. I'm thinking about what his dad might have packed for him today when I notice Trevor, Brice and the rest of the guys return to eating their lunches as though I were invisible. "Four left," I say, trying to get their attention. "Two Twix and two Milky Ways. Who wants 'em?" I waggle the candy bars.

Nobody looks up.

Weird.

Trevor lifts an eyebrow, then quickly goes back to eating his lunch.

That's when I get it. Someone's standing behind me. I can almost feel the heat from the person, centimeters from my back.

I turn, and when I look up and see who it is, the bottom drops out of my stomach.

Some French courtiers used soft cloth as toilet paper; others used goose feathers. Because feathers didn't provide the leverage needed to wipe one's bottom, some people used feathers still attached to the neck of the dead goose!

Mr. Sheffield, vice principal in charge of discipline, towers over me, lips knife-thin and nostrils flared.

I've never been to Mr. Sheffield's office, but everyone knows he's the guy who breaks up fights, gives out detention slips and suspends kids. I heard that if you do something really bad, he can even get you sent to juvie. *I wish Angus Andrews would get sent to juvie so I wouldn't have to stand near him and his stinky armpits in the locker room anymore.*

I grip my four candy bars a little too tightly.

"What do we have here?" Mr. Sheffield asks in a deep voice, but I can tell he doesn't expect an answer. He's asking a *rhetorical* question. In this case, "rhetorical" means I'm in huge trouble!

Delaney Phillips stands beside Mr. Sheffield, smiling, but not her nice high-wattage smile that sometimes makes my cheeks feel warm. She's sporting an evil smile that goes well with Mr. Sheffield's tight-lipped scowl.

"See, I told you, Mr. Sheffield," Delaney says, crossing her arms.

"You may go back to your seat now, Miss Phillips," Mr. Sheffield says in a quiet voice.

Quiet voices are sometimes scarier than loud ones.

I watch Delaney strut back to her lunch table, like she just brought the late uber-criminal Al Capone to justice or something.

"Hand it over," Mr. Sheffield says, holding out his unnaturally large palm.

At first, I think Mr. Sheffield wants me to hand over the money I earned today, and my heart goes into overdrive, because there's nearly a hundred dollars in my backpack— our rent money. And Mr. Katz is coming today to collect. So there's no way I'm handing that over. Even to Mr. Sheffield. Even to keep from getting suspended. Or thrown into juvie.

Since I'm holding four slightly smooshed candy bars, I place them on Mr. Sheffield's outstretched hand.

He wraps his fingers around the candy and motions for me to follow him.

"Ooooh!" kids taunt as I walk out of the cafeteria.

Delaney looks over at me, a satisfied smirk on her face.

Traitor! What have I ever done to you, Delaney Phillips, but admire you and buy your lousy Golly Pops?

Toothpick catches my eye. He looks like he feels sorry for me. I feel sorry for me, because Toothpick's eating a gigantic sandwich that is probably filled with delicious things and I won't be able to help him finish it.

• • •

In Mr. Sheffield's small, messy office, I sit in one of two chairs facing his desk, which is covered with papers and file folders.

"Name?" he asks, focusing on his computer screen.

I consider giving a fake name or someone else's name—like Angus Andrews—but simply squeak, "Benjamin Epstein." Then I silently pray, *Please don't call my mom.* For once, I'm glad she doesn't have a phone, but I know she gave the school Mrs. Schneckle's number in case of emergency.

Mr. Sheffield types, and I sink lower in my chair. *What if he does call, and Mrs. Schneckle goes to Mom's work to tell her? Mom can't take off from work.*

He nods at the screen, then turns to me. "Apparently, Mr. Epstein, you fancy yourself an enterprising entrepreneur."

The words feel like a compliment, so I allow myself a small smile.

"But you can't sell candy on school grounds."

My smile disintegrates.

"In fact . . ." He presses his palms on his desk and leans toward me. "You can't sell *anything* on school grounds. Do I make myself abundantly clear, Mr. Epstein?"

I swallow hard and nod, but I know this isn't fair. Before I can stop it, words explode from my mouth: "Delaney Phillips sells Golly Pops. That's candy."

Mr. Sheffield lets out a breath. "She's supposed to sell candy, Mr. Epstein. It's a school-sanctioned project to support the band's upcoming trip to Hershey." He pushes his glasses up on his nose, and for some reason, I do the same with my glasses. "No one's buying from her, Mr. Epstein, or from any of the other band kids, because they're buying your candy bars." He taps one of my four slightly smooshed candy bars lying on his desk. "Can we have that happen, Mr. Epstein?"

I shake my head to show Mr. Sheffield I agree with him, even though I don't. It's not my fault the candy I sell tastes better than Golly Pops and people would rather spend their money on them. *That's capitalism for you, Mr. Sheffield.* Besides, the reason I need to sell candy bars is way more important than the band kids going on a dopey trip to Hershey.

"I see by your file from last year that you're a good kid, Mr. Epstein—excellent grades, never in trouble."

I nod and swallow hard.

"So I'm going to let you walk out of here with a warning."

I let out the breath I didn't realize I was holding. "Thank you." Then, even though I feel dumb, I say, "Sir."

"Don't thank me." Mr. Sheffield points at me. "Watch yourself. If I catch you selling anything on school grounds again—anything!—I'll not only confiscate it, I'll suspend you. Got it?"

My throat constricts, but I manage to squeeze out one syllable: "Yes."

"Okay, then." Mr. Sheffield drops my four melting candy bars into his trash can. "Get to class, Mr. Epstein."

"Yes sir!"

I run toward PE, then remember the rule about not running in the halls and slow to a fast walk.

When I reach the locker room, it's so late everyone is already in the gym except Angus Andrews. He's in the same row, only three lockers away from mine, and I can smell his stinky armpits even though we haven't even had gym yet.

I yank off my regular clothes and throw on my gym clothes in record time. Then I remember there's nearly a hundred dollars in my backpack. I glance at Angus and shove the backpack into my locker.

"Got any more?" Angus asks, stepping closer.

The little hairs on my forearms stand at attention. "More what?" I ask, slamming my locker door and spinning the lock.

Angus nods toward my locker. "You're the kid selling candy bars. Right?"

Those are more words than Angus Andrews has ever spoken to me. "Was selling them. Not anymore."

Angus puts his foot on the bench next to me, and I fight the urge to step backward. "Why not? 'Cause Sheffield told you to stop? I heard what happened in the cafeteria."

"You did?"

Angus nods. "He won't do anything to you."

"Huh?"

"Sheffield. He won't really do anything. I should know." Angus laughs, but nothing is funny.

"Maybe you're right." I stumble out of the locker room, hoping Angus doesn't find a way to break into my locker and steal my money while I'm in the gym.

The moment my sneaker touches the gym floor, Coach yells, "You're late! Give me ten laps."

I'm almost glad to run around the perimeter of the gym while everyone else practices setting and spiking the volleyball. It gives me time to think, to figure things out and relieve the stress of being in such close proximity to Angus Andrews.

Angus is an idiot, but maybe he has a point. Maybe Mr. Sheffield won't do anything to me. I'm a good kid who never gets in trouble. But I'm on his radar now, and he did threaten to suspend me. I can't get suspended. That would hurt Mom too much.

Then I remember exactly what Mr. Sheffield said in his office: "If I catch you."

What if he doesn't catch me?

But what if he does? Or if Delaney Phillips rats me out again?

I'll have to come up with another plan. Maybe I can sell my spleen after all. I wonder how much spleens go for these days. I wish the Royal-T contest were sooner, but the deadline isn't until October second, a whole week from now, and they still need time to choose the winner after that.

What else could I possibly do to earn a lot of money right away?

I can't sell my other winnings from the prize closet. No one wants to buy lame T-shirts and baseball caps with company names on them.

As I pound around the perimeter of the gym, I notice Angus Andrews slip out from the locker room and join a game of volleyball, completely unnoticed by Coach.

How does he do that?

Jogging the rest of my humiliation laps, I hope Mom's gotten some amazingly generous tips the past couple days.

After PE, I hurry to the locker room to make sure my backpack is still in my locker with the money inside. It is. But I know that even though almost two hundred dollars is a ton of money for me, it's not nearly enough for Mr. Katz. And today he's going to ask for the rest of the money we owe. I hope there's a grand-prize check from some sweepstakes or contest waiting for me in the mailbox at home.

I hope . . .

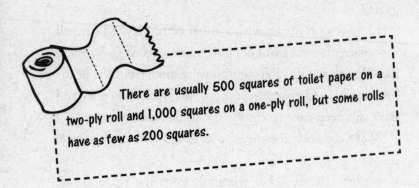

There are usually 500 squares of toilet paper on a two-ply roll and 1,000 squares on a one-ply roll, but some rolls have as few as 200 squares.

As usual, I touch Dad's name on our mailbox for luck, but it doesn't work, because there's only one thing inside the slim metal box: the *Sweeps-a-Lot* newsletter, which arrives twice a month. Aunt Abby buys me an annual subscription every year for my birthday.

The newsletter was not what I was hoping for, but it is a lot of fun to look through.

Its pages are loaded with opportunities to win fun trips, free merchandise, new cars and amazing cash prizes. When the newsletter arrives, I have a hard time paying attention to anything else, especially unimportant things like homework, because I can't wait to read about all the cool prizes I could win.

Of course, I'd be able to enjoy it a lot more today if I weren't worried about Mr. Katz showing up and us not having all the money we're supposed to pay him.

I drop my cash-filled backpack on the couch, grateful Mr. Sheffield didn't call Mom. But I'm going to have to tell her where I'm getting all this money. I hope she'll be happy, not angry.

I take the newsletter to the table. From my shoe box full of sweepstakes supplies, I pull out a yellow and a blue highlighter—yellow for online sweeps I want to enter and blue for mail-in sweeps that look promising. I'll enter the online sweeps at Toothpick's house or at the library. I'm careful about which mail-in sweeps I choose, because each one requires a stamp, and those things add up. Luckily, I still have stamps from my "payment" for helping Toothpick film and clean up after *Guess Who We're Having for Dinner*.

I'm devouring the *Sweeps-a-Lot* "Page Two Profile" about Adeline Patchett from Memphis, Tennessee—who's won eleven trips, two cars and over $28,000 in cash during her twenty-six years of sweeping—when Mom walks in.

"Hey there."

"Hi." My stomach flops, because I know I'm going to give Mom the money from my backpack and it's still not going to be enough. Maybe her tips were great this week. I cross my fingers under the table.

Mom drops into her chair with a thud, like her body weighs a thousand pounds. "Tips have been extra lousy this week," she says, closing her eyelids.

"Oh."

Two minutes later, there's a sharp knock at the door.

"Here we go." Mom runs a hand through her hair, then pushes up from the table.

I clutch my newsletter as Mom opens the door.

Mr. Katz's voice makes my heart hammer, and Dad's words swirl around my mind. I know I have to do something.

When Mom goes toward her bedroom, I grab my backpack and run into my room. I gather all the money I've made—almost two hundred dollars—but something makes me hold out fifty bucks and stash it in the bag in my underwear drawer. Just in case.

I intercept Mom in the hallway, on her way back to Mr. Katz. She has only one envelope—marked *Rent*—in her hand. I'm relieved she still hasn't touched the Grand Plan money.

"Here," I say, shoving a fat stack of one-dollar bills at her. "It's almost a hundred and fifty dollars."

Mom's eyes go wide, and she whispers fiercely, "Benjamin, where did you get this money?"

I swallow hard, thinking of Mr. Sheffield telling me I shouldn't have been selling them. "I sold candy bars."

"What? How?"

"I bought candy bars from WaWa for fifty cents each and sold them at school for a dollar each." I think of how heavy the bags were. "Lots of candy bars."

"They let you do that at school?"

My cheeks heat up. I don't want to tell Mom what happened with Mr. Sheffield today. I don't want her to know he threatened to suspend me. "Apparently—"

"Hello?" Mr. Katz yells through the open door. "Are you coming?"

"Thank you, sweetheart," Mom says, gripping my money tightly. "I'll pay you back. Every last dollar." Then Mom touches my cheek and looks hard into my eyes. "With your money and my tips since Monday, we have about three fifty to give Mr. Katz. It's not the eighteen hundred we owe, but it's something." Mom takes a deep breath. "Then we'll owe only fourteen fifty. Only!" Mom laughs like a hyena, but nothing is funny.

When she steps outside our apartment with Mr. Katz, I sit at the table and look over my Royal-T slogans again. *Pamper. Damper. Hamper.*

Mom comes in, shuts the door and returns to the table. "We tried, Benjamin."

"Tried?"

Mom pats my hand, which annoys me for some reason. "He said it wasn't enough. And next month's rent will be due in less than a week."

"What's he going to do?" I ask.

"He said his hands were tied. Said his business partner was breathing down his neck."

"Eviction?" I ask.

"Eviction," she says. And the word sounds so final. "He's going to file papers."

"What are we going to—"

"This is what we're going to do," Mom says, pulling a twenty-dollar bill from her pocket. "We're going to the Country Club Diner for dinner."

"Huh?"

"Some customer gave me a twenty-dollar tip for a cup of coffee and a single pancake. I tucked it away, and we're going to use it to celebrate."

"Celebrate?" Now I know Mom's totally lost it. This feels like something Dad would have done. He was always "celebrating" dumb things, like the fact that I cleared my plate without being asked or said "Good morning" in just the right way. With Dad, just about anything would be an occasion to break out the fixings for an ice cream sundae or go out for a soft pretzel or a water ice at Rita's.

Mom sits taller. "We'll celebrate the fact that I have the most awesome kid in the universe." She ruffles my hair with her knuckles, and it feels like she's digging through my scalp to my brain. "Thinking of selling those candy bars to help out. My own little entrepreneur."

I like the way Mom says it. She means it as a compliment, not like when Mr. Sheffield called me an entrepreneur and it sounded like I was a criminal.

"Hey, how did you get the money to buy the candy bars in the first place?"

"Finally sold that Genie's Genius grill that was in my closet. Some guy bought it for sixty bucks."

"Some guy?"

"We did it through SellSpace and met him in a busy public place."

"Still." Mom gives me that parenting look that means I shouldn't have done that; then she says something that surprises me: "Best. Kid. In. The. Universe!"

I think of the universe Dad painted on my ceiling and I smile from Mom's compliment.

"We'll go as soon as I take a shower. I smell like bacon."

I grab my *Sweeps-a-Lot* newsletter and jump into Dad's recliner while I wait for Mom. I should get homework done before we leave, but it's more fun to scour the newsletter and choose the sweepstakes I want to enter.

Curled up in Dad's recliner, with the shower running in the background, I allow myself to imagine winning the biggest prizes listed in the newsletter: cash, trips and cars.

I'm going to win a grand prize soon. I can feel it.

I'm still thinking about winning a grand prize when we get to the Country Club Diner.

We each end up ordering a hot veggie hoagie, and we get a slice of lemon meringue pie—Dad's favorite—to share for dessert.

"So how did you come up with the idea to sell candy bars?" Mom asks, putting her napkin on her lap.

"Delaney Phillips was selling Golly Pops to raise money for a band trip to Hershey. I thought kids would rather buy candy bars."

"Hmm. I hope you didn't cut into Delaney's sales."

I'm silent, praying Mom changes the subject.

"Benjamin, I can't wait to take the test and start working at Mr. Daniels's firm. I talked to him recently and found out I'll be earning more than twice what I make now. Everything will be so much easier for us."

"That'll be great, Mom. When can you take the test?"

"The minute I get confirmation in the mail, I'll schedule it. And it takes only about a week or two to get the results after that. We'll have to hang in there a little longer."

I'm trying.

"Hey, what should we do tomorrow after I get done with work? It's Saturday. We should do something fun."

I look out the window at the parking lot.

"Want to visit Dad?" she asks.

My chest tightens at the thought of going to the cemetery and seeing Dad's name on the gravestone. "That's not fun," I say quietly.

"You're right," Mom says. "Of course not. What was I thinking? We'll go some other time. What about taking a walk through Pennypack Park?"

That doesn't sound like fun either. "Sounds great."

"And Sunday?" Mom asks, taking a sip of water. "After I get home from work, why don't we plan to clean the apartment. Then you can do homework and I'll study?"

"Now, that sounds exciting," I say, as though she's just told me we're flying on a rocket ship to the moon.

"Yeah." Mom waves her straw. "I know. A thrill a minute. But it's got to get done."

Our waitress comes over with our hoagies and puts the

slice of pie in the center of the table. "Can I get you two anything else?"

My dad.

And a Sunday that won't be a big pile of boring.

"No, we're fine," Mom says.

And her words hang in the air like a lie-filled rain cloud.

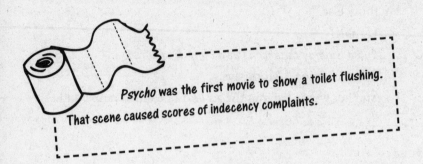

Psycho was the first movie to show a toilet flushing. That scene caused scores of indecency complaints.

Sunday, it turns out, is *not* a big pile of boring.

Mom and I are at the table. She's studying for the CPA exam, and I'm filling out contest entries, imagining someone coming to our door to deliver a huge grand prize. I'm also working on my Royal-T slogan but can't come up with anything great.

"What do you want for dinner?" Mom asks.

I know there's nothing much in the house, so I say, "Whatever."

"How about—"

There's a knock at the door.

Mom tenses.

I feel like telling Mom to relax. It's probably someone

delivering a contest win to Shelley B. Epstein. In fact, I'm feeling so positive that I go to the door and fling it open.

"Ben, you need to ask who—"

"Zeyde?" I'm staring at my slightly disheveled grandfather, who's holding a suitcase in one hand and a pizza box in the other.

"Boychik!" Zeyde shouts.

"Dad?" Mom rushes over and grabs the suitcase from Zeyde's hand.

I take the pizza box and push my contest stuff out of the way so I can put it on the table.

"What . . . why . . . ?" Mom leads Zeyde to the couch. "Where's Abby? Why are you here? I thought . . ." She turns to me. "Go get your *zeyde* a glass of water."

I run into the kitchen, fill up a glass and run back. I don't want to miss anything.

Zeyde downs the water in a few gulps, hands me the glass and opens his arms. "How are my two favorite Philadelphians?"

I put the glass in the sink, then sit in Dad's recliner, cross my legs and lean forward.

"How did you get here? Why . . . ?" Mom takes one of Zeyde's veiny hands. "You're supposed to be in Florida, Dad. With Abby."

"Did you walk back here?" I ask.

Mom shoots me a look that tells me my question was both idiotic and annoying.

Zeyde reaches over and pats my knee. "Benjamin, your

zeyde is in pretty amazing shape for an old geezer, but not amazing enough to walk twelve hundred miles. With a suitcase. I took a cab. The bill's four thousand dollars. The guy's waiting outside to get paid."

Mom's mouth opens, but no sound comes out.

"I'm joking, Shelley!"

She forgets to laugh.

"I took a cab to the airport in West Palm Beach and got a good seat on the plane," Zeyde says. "After landing in Philly, I hailed a cab and made the driver stop at Kirk's Pizza." He winks at me. "Ben's favorite."

I smell the delicious pizza sitting on the table, and my mouth waters.

"But why?" Mom asks.

Zeyde pulls his hand from Mom's grip and rubs it over his bald head. "Did you know your sister has fourteen cats, Shelley? Fourteen *meshugge* cats!"

I didn't know that. When we visited her a while ago, she had only four: Kiwi, Avocado, Jasmine and Fred. Fred was the smallest and the bossiest.

"Do you know how a tiny two-bedroom condo smells with fourteen cats in it?"

I think Zeyde's asking a rhetorical question and doesn't expect us to answer. In this case, "rhetorical" probably means super-sized stink-o-rama! Sometimes Toothpick's cat, Psycho, smells up the whole house when she poops. I can't imagine that odor times fourteen!

"Your sister's turned into a crazy cat lady, Shelley!"

Mom bursts out laughing, then covers her mouth. "This is not good," she says. "Does Abby even know you left?"

"Of course." Zeyde looks at his shoes. "Well . . ."

"Dad?" Mom gives Zeyde the look that's like truth serum pouring out of her eyeballs. You can't tell a lie when Mom gives you *that* look.

"Abby may not be entirely aware that I left today. But she knew I was going to leave soon. We talked about it a few days ago. I told her I was going to come and stay with you guys for a while. At least, I think it was a few days ago."

"And?" Mom asks.

"And," Zeyde continues, "when I woke this morning, there was a cat on my head." He pats his bald head. "On. My. Head!"

"Oh my." Mom slaps a hand over her mouth.

"That's when I decided to fly here." Zeyde looks around. "You don't have any cats here, do you?"

"Nope," I answer. "Just Barkley."

Zeyde tilts his head. "Who?"

I know he's joking, because every time Zeyde visits, he always goes into my room to say hello to Barkley. And last Chanukah, he bought Barkley a castle to go inside his tank. Dad died shortly before Chanukah. I remember feeling miserable that Dad didn't get to see Barkley's new castle. Or light the candles with us. Or eat latkes with applesauce— his favorite dish.

"Barkley," I say. "You know. My betta fish."

Zeyde looks confused, but then shakes his head and

keeps talking. "I half think Abby got all those cats just so I wouldn't want to live there."

"I'm sure she didn't, Dad. I hadn't realized she had that many, though."

I'm a little freaked out that Zeyde doesn't know who Barkley is. He wasn't in Florida *that* long!

"We'd better call Abby and let her know you're all right."

"After we eat." Zeyde pats my knee. "Pizza's getting cold, and I'm hungry."

"Let's call first," Mom says. "I don't want Abby to worry."

"I missed you, Shelley. And Ben, too. How's an old geezer like me supposed to go so long without seeing my favorite Philadelphians?"

"We missed you, too, Dad, but you were there only three weeks. You were supposed to stay the whole winter, then come back here in the summer for a vacation. You agreed to this. Remember?"

Zeyde lets out a big breath. "Did I mention the cats? Fourteen of them. No normal person has fourteen cats, Shelley. She had only six last time I was there. Only. Listen to me. I'm becoming meshugge like your sister!"

"Oh, Dad." Mom gives Zeyde a hug, then pulls back. "Give me your cell. I'm going to call Abby to let her know what's going on."

"She knows," he says. "I told you. Bring over my suitcase, Ben."

I grab it. "It's heavy."

"I know. Your old *zeyde* has too much stuff." He opens the suitcase and pulls out a box. "Abby gave me this for you, Shelley. She said it's all taken care of and you'd need one if you had me. Whatever that means."

"A cell phone," I say and pump my fist in the air. *Finally. A phone.* It's been three long months since we couldn't afford to pay the phone bill. Mom uses Mrs. Schneckle's phone if she needs to make a call, and I use it if I need to call Toothpick. *Embarrassing.*

Mom examines the new phone, then dials. "Abby?"

Zeyde leans back on the couch, closing his eyelids.

"Yes, he's here," Mom says. "He's fine."

There's a pause.

"Of course, but—"

Another pause.

"I know, but—"

Then Mom whispers, "He's been taking his memory medicine, right?"

"Yes, he has," Zeyde says, his eyelids still closed. "And he's not deaf."

I chuckle.

Mom covers the phone and says, "Benjamin, take your *zeyde*'s suitcase to your room."

I stop chuckling. "My room?" I whisper. "Zeyde's staying with me?" I know it makes sense because I have the extra bed in there, and I love him and all, but I'm not sure I'm ready for a roommate who has wrinkles the size of the

Grand Canyon on his forehead and one really annoying thing that I discovered when I slept over Zeyde's a while ago, something that *kept* me from sleeping!

"Now," Mom says, clearly irritated.

I haul Zeyde's suitcase into my room and heave it onto the daybed, then look up at the stars and comets, as though the universe will somehow give me an answer.

It doesn't.

Barkley is nonplussed by the whole thing, swimming in and out of his castle as though nothing has just changed. "You're getting a new roommate," I tell him. "And he snores!"

Barkley doesn't seem distressed by the news.

When I return to the living room/dining room/kitchen, I hear Mom say, "I'll call you later. Thanks for the phone, Abs." Mom looks at me. "We really appreciate it." Mom pushes a button and sighs. "Well, anyone besides me hungry?"

I eat four slices of pizza, and on each of them I sprinkle red pepper flakes from a basket of spices I won from the Spice It Up with Spandex Sweepstakes.

"If it's too much, Shelley, I can stay at a motel or something," Zeyde says, wiping sauce from his chin.

I think of the Bates Motel from that scary movie Toothpick showed me once. "You shouldn't stay at a motel. It's not a good idea."

"No, not a good idea," Mom says, smiling at me. "Besides, motels cost money, and last time I checked, you're not Donald Trump."

"Of course I'm not Donald Trump," Zeyde says. "He has hair."

"And money," Mom points out.

Zeyde looks at his lap. "I just don't want to be in the way, Shelley."

"You're not in the way," I tell him, even though my room will be really crowded with another person. "We can play cards, and when I'm at school, Barkley will keep you company."

"Who?" Zeyde says again.

Mom gets that worry wrinkle between her eyebrows. "You sure you're taking your medicine, Dad?"

"Every day," Zeyde says, tapping his head. "Working better than ever."

"If you say so," Mom says, but I can tell she's not convinced.

After dinner, Mom pulls out her book to study for the CPA exam, but I can tell she's not really studying, because she's staring off into the distance. I do my homework but stop to think about Zeyde moving in here, sharing my room and being confused about Barkley. *Did he really not know who he was? Or was he joking around?*

Zeyde's in the bathroom when Mom asks, "Benjamin, are you okay with Zeyde moving in here for a while? I know things were easier when he had his own apartment, but Aunt Abby and I were afraid to have him living alone. You know, with his memory problems."

"It'll be fine," I say. "We can do, you know, guy stuff."

"Yeah." Mom bites her bottom lip. "I hope it works out. See, Aunt Abby was supposed to—"

The bathroom door clicks opens, and Mom stops talking.

Zeyde strides into the living room/dining room/kitchen and slams a roll of gray, scratchy toilet paper onto the table. "Shelley, please," Zeyde pleads. "Have a little sympathy for an old man's *tuchis*." Then he reaches into his pocket and pulls out a ten-dollar bill and slaps it onto the table next to the toilet paper. "I'm begging you. Buy some decent toilet paper."

I run to my closet and return with a fluffy roll of Royal-T—from the free four-pack Mom picked up at the ACME. I'm saving the rest of the rolls for an emergency. I can almost hear Toothpick mocking me, saying *A toilet paper emergency?* and punching me in the arm for being a total moron.

Zeyde rubs the Royal-T toilet paper against his cheek. "Ah," he says. "That's better. No splinters in this stuff."

Mom's shoulders bob, and I think she's crying because she feels bad that we can afford only lousy toilet paper, but then she bursts out laughing.

I laugh, too.

Zeyde laughs hard, then stops suddenly. He pushes his false teeth back in. "Oh my," he says, tears leaking out of the corners of his eyes. "Almost lost my teeth on that one."

This makes Mom hysterical.

And Zeyde keeps chuckling, but softly. I can tell he's afraid he's going to lose his teeth again, because he's got his hand over his mouth.

I'm bent over from laughing so hard, and my stomach hurts in a good way. I can't wait to tell Toothpick about Zeyde's teeth flying out.

Laughter sounds great in our apartment. Much better than Mr. Katz's awful word: "eviction." It reminds me of how our apartment sounded when Dad was still here, before he got sick and everything.

I'm definitely going to enjoy having Zeyde here.

Dear Mr. Ed Chase,

Congratulations. You have another fan of your toilet paper.

Zeyde Jake, my grandfather, moved here from Florida. He said he couldn't live with my aunt Abby's fourteen cats, but I can't imagine her having that many. Maybe Zeyde counted wrong. He didn't even remember who Barkley was.

But that's not important now.

The important thing is Zeyde.

He's here and he made my mom laugh so hard when his teeth almost fell out. It's not always easy to make my mom laugh these days. And Zeyde's teeth are fine, so don't worry.

Now that Zeyde's here, maybe things will work out with the rent and all. At least I hope so. We're running out of time.

Thanks for always being there to write to.

Your friend,
Benjamin Epstein

P.S. Q: What is tuna fish + tuna fish?
A: Tuna fish + tuna fish = Fourna fish
(That was one of my dad's dumb jokes. Fishy, right? Ha ha.)

In ancient Rome, public bathrooms contained a bucket of salt water into which a sponge on a stick had been placed. A person used the sponge to wipe, then put it back in the bucket for the next person.

Before bed, I use Mom's new cell phone to call Toothpick.

"You got a phone?" Pick asks.

"Yeah. It's from my aunt Abby."

"Dude, that's awesome!"

I don't tell Pick the phone is actually Mom's and I'm only borrowing it.

"Guess who showed up at our door tonight, carrying a pizza?"

"No idea."

"My *zeyde*."

"Zeyde Jake's there? I thought he moved to Florida or something a few weeks ago."

"He did, but now he's here. He brought pizza from Kirk's and a suitcase."

"Is he going to live with you guys?"

"I guess. For a while."

"Cool. Maybe we can put him in our next horror film."

I think of the tufts of hair growing from Zeyde's ears. "He'd be perfect. You should have seen what happened tonight. He can pop his teeth out of his mouth and—" I hear someone walking down the hall toward my bedroom. "Gotta go."

My bedroom door opens. "Hi, Mom."

Her hand is out, as though she's waiting for me to put something in it.

I drop the phone into her palm. "I just called Toothpick."

"That's fine. You can use the phone anytime you want. That was really nice of Aunt Abby, wasn't it?"

"Really nice," I say.

"I miss her."

"Me too," I say. "I wish we could visit her again." But then I feel bad, because Mom probably wishes that, too, but we don't even have enough money to pay our stupid rent, much less to fly to Florida for a vacation.

Mom sits on the edge of my bed and lets out a big breath. "Well, that was a surprise."

For a second, I wonder what she's talking about, but then I see Zeyde's suitcase and know she's talking about him showing up at our door.

"Big surprise," I say. "But I'm glad it was Zeyde at the door and not Mr. Katz."

This makes Mom smile. "You sure you're okay bunking with Zeyde?"

"Totally. It'll be awesome."

"You're the best, Benjamin." Mom kisses my forehead. "G'night, sweetheart."

"Night, Mom."

She taps on the tank. "G'night to you, too, Barkley. You're sure lucky to have Ben looking after you."

I want to tell Mom it's not good to tap on the glass, but she's been so stressed that I don't say anything. Maybe I'll put a little sign up on Barkley's tank about not tapping on the glass, like they do in pet stores.

After Mom leaves, I try to read my history textbook, but I'm zonked, so I switch off the desk lamp, roll toward the wall and close my eyelids.

Zeyde wakes me when he comes into the bedroom and says, "Good toilet paper, Benjamin."

Even though it's a weird thing for someone to say, it makes me smile.

I hear Zeyde put something on the desk between our beds, but I'm too tired to roll over to see what it is.

The daybed squeaks, and Zeyde lets out a little groan.

"Good night," I say quietly.

"Good night, Mary."

My heart races. I want to rocket up and tell Mom what Zeyde just said, because Mary is the name of my *bubbe*— Zeyde's wife.

And she died three years ago.

"I'm not Mary," I whisper. "I'm Ben." When I don't hear anything, I add, "Your grandson."

Zeyde doesn't say a word, and for a second I panic that he's dead, but then I hear loud breathing.

First, Zeyde doesn't remember Barkley; then he forgets who I am. *What's going on?*

"Zeyde?" I whisper.

A soft grunt.

"Please be okay."

I roll over toward him and blink to help my eyes adjust in the darkness. But without my glasses, all I see is a long lump under the covers in the daybed. The lump rumbles every few seconds.

Then the lump's rumbles intensify.

Soon Zeyde sounds like the trash truck that groans and grumbles down the driveway behind our apartment building.

"Zeyde," I whisper fiercely, my throat dry as sand because I'm so thirsty from Kirk's Pizza and those Spice It Up with Spandex red pepper flakes. "You're snoring!"

He doesn't hear me over the sound of his snoring.

Next thing I know, Zeyde's snores escalate to lawn-mower proportions.

"Seriously?" I flip onto my back. *How am I supposed to sleep with a lawn mower in the next bed?*

I wouldn't have believed it was possible, but Zeyde Jake's snores get even louder. Now he sounds like a jackhammer—um, Jakehammer—breaking through cement. I expect Mom to burst in, telling Zeyde she needs her sleep for work.

But she doesn't.

She's probably sleeping blissfully through the noise in the next room.

Once, when we visited Aunt Abby during a category 1 hurricane, Mom was the only one who slept through it. Aunt Abby, Dad, me and even the cats were awake, watching through the sliding glass door as palm trees dipped and swayed through wild sheets of rain.

Just when I think Zeyde's snores can't possibly get louder, they ramp up to earthquake level. It feels like my bed is actually shaking. I'm pretty sure if Zeyde's snores *were* an earthquake, they'd register at least 6.5 on the Richter scale and be felt throughout Philadelphia and maybe the rest of Pennsylvania, too.

I consider stuffing Royal-T into my ears to block the Zeyde-quake, but I don't want to waste it. Maybe Zeyde staying in my room isn't the best idea. Maybe I can sleep at Toothpick's while he's here. Maybe I need Mom to buy me industrial-strength earplugs or something.

While I'm lying there, having my eardrums blasted by Zeyde's seismic snores, a word wiggles into my brain and brings a mountain of worry with it: "eviction." I wish I could stop thinking about it, but I can't. No matter what else is going on, the worry hangs over it. Mom and I never really talked about what Mr. Katz said about filing eviction papers. We never talked about what we were going to do to keep that from happening.

I look at the lump that is my snoring *zeyde*.

If we get kicked out now, we'll have Zeyde with us, too. I dread the thought of the three of us *having* to live with Aunt Abby and her fourteen cats. Barkley might end up a fish feast for one of her furry felines! But then I relax a little, because I realize Zeyde will probably be able to help pay the rest of what we owe for rent. At least, I hope he can.

I look at Barkley in the dim light from the streetlamp and say, "Must be nice to have someone take care of you all the time and never have to worry about anything."

Barkley doesn't answer me.

Fish are stubborn like that.

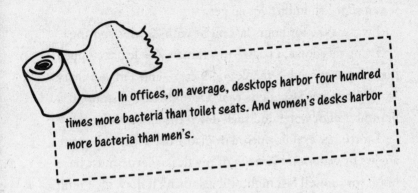

In offices, on average, desktops harbor four hundred times more bacteria than toilet seats. And women's desks harbor more bacteria than men's.

When I wake in the morning, I'm too tired to lift the drywall that my eyelids have become. I want to lie in bed until they return to normal eyelid weight, but the alarm under my pillow won't stop jangling. It's not loud, but it's annoying, so I reach under and turn it off.

It's Monday, the twenty-eighth of September. That means I have to get up for school.

It also means we have three days until the rent is due again. On October 1, we'll owe another $1,200 in addition to the $1,450 we already owe! I can't deal with those numbers right now.

Five more minutes, I think, but I know I need to get up,

so I reach for my eyeglasses. When I don't feel them, I take it as a sign I shouldn't get up yet.

I was awake for hours last night with Zeyde's snoring.

Lying facedown, I realize two things: Zeyde has stopped his seismic snoring—thank goodness!—and I'm so thirsty from the pizza last night that I could stick a straw in a bathtub full of water and suck down the entire thing.

I force my eyelids open. I'm glad I do, because I notice a glass of water on the edge of my desk. Zeyde must have left it for himself last night. I'll just drink it now, then refill it later for him. I'm sure he won't mind.

Sitting up, I grab the glass and gulp down the contents, thinking I'll need a dozen more of these before my thirst is quenched.

Mental alarm bells clang as I'm drinking. Something's wrong. Bad wrong! Before my brain can make sense of what I just did, I'm lips-to-dentures with Zeyde's false teeth. And the liquid I gulped was not plain water. It tasted like baking soda, which I tasted once when Toothpick's mom was making cookies. The glass must have been filled with Zeyde's denture cleaner and all the crud that came off his teeth last night, while they were soaking.

"Ack! ACK! ACK!"

The gagging won't stop, and the frantic thought *My lips just touched Zeyde's false teeth. Does this mean I kissed his dentures?* "ACK!" I swipe at my tongue like a maniac and do what any self-respecting seventh-grade guy would: I hurl partially digested pizza chunks onto my comforter in a long stream of vomit. Kirk's Pizza sure doesn't taste as good coming up as it did going down. "ACK!"

Zeyde shoots straight up. "What the—"

I'm sputtering and wiping my mouth on the edge of the comforter. "Ugh," I moan.

"What the— Where am— What's that smell?" But Zeyde's words don't sound right. I focus on him, squint and see his lips collapsed over his gums. His mouth looks too small for his face.

I slide the glass containing his teeth toward his side of the desk.

He pops his teeth into his mouth without washing them off, even though they touched my lips. I feel like I might hurl all over again.

"What happened?" Zeyde asks, fumbling for and finding his eyeglasses.

"Please," I say, "don't ever—ever!—EVER!—leave your dentures near my bed. Keep them in the bathroom or something." I swipe at my lips with the back of my hand.

Zeyde slaps a palm over his mouth, and his shoulders jerk. At first I think he's having a seizure or something, then I realize he's laughing. At me! I'm sitting with a stinking pile of pizza vomit in my lap, and Zeyde is practically hysterical.

"Thanks," I say, capturing the vomit in my comforter by folding over the edges.

"Sorry, Ben," Zeyde says, his shoulders still bobbing. "Did you really drink my . . . Oh my!" He wipes the corner

— 83 —

of each eye to keep tears of laughter from streaming down his cheeks, I guess. "That's funny."

"This," I say, holding the bunched-up comforter, "isn't funny." My mouth tastes like acid, and my throat burns.

"No, it's really not." Zeyde's still chuckling, though. He stands, stretches and yanks his green Eagles sweatshirt over his head—being careful of his eyeglasses—then gathers my comforter and pillow in a heap. "I'll take this down to the laundry room." He pokes his gnarled feet into bedroom slippers while I find my own glasses.

"You don't have to," I say. "I can get it." But really, I think Zeyde should clean it because it was his fault I hurled.

With the bundle under his arm, Zeyde looks back over his shoulder at me. "Get yourself to school," he says. "That's more important. I'll take care of this." Then he looks at my desk. "Hey, Barkley. How you doin', old pal?"

Barkley, oblivious to my trauma, swims happily around his tank, in and out of the castle Zeyde bought him.

I let out a breath, happy Zeyde knows who Barkley is this morning. He must have just had a bad day yesterday. Maybe traveling made him a little confused or something. I'm glad he's better now.

"Hey," Zeyde says. "Maybe I'll meet that Mrs. Schneckle while I'm down there. She's a good egg. Isn't she?"

"Yup," I say. "And she makes a mean peach kugel." I try to make Zeyde smile so he'll know I forgive him for leaving his dentures within drinking range.

"I like kugel," Zeyde says, rubbing a hand over his stomach. "Your aunt Abby wouldn't let me eat anything like that. Said it wasn't good for my cholesterol level." Zeyde waves his free hand dismissively. "Eh! *Farkakt* cholesterol!"

"Zeyde!"

He shrugs. "'Cholesterol' isn't a bad word." Then he winks.

Secretly, I'm glad Zeyde talks to me like he would a grown-up, but I'm also glad Mom's at work and doesn't hear. I grab Zeyde a packet of laundry detergent from the shelf in the bathroom. "It's the cheap stuff, but . . ."

He pushes his glasses up on his nose and examines the packet. "It'll do the job."

I look at Zeyde—wearing sweatpants, an Eagles sweatshirt and slippers—starting his day by carrying my vomit-filled comforter to our gross laundry room, and I know he's a good guy, even if he does snore like an earthquake and have combable ear hair. "Thanks, Zeyde."

"Thank you, Benjamin." He nods. "I'm sure it's not easy having an old fart like me share your bedroom."

"It's no big deal," I say. "Just keep your teeth in the bathroom from now on."

Zeyde nods. "Teeth in the bathroom. Or in my mouth."

After Zeyde leaves the apartment, I go to the bathroom and brush my teeth about ten times, but still, while I'm walking to school, my mouth tastes like acidy pizza vomit.

It's not until I'm in the cafeteria for lunch that I realize

I haven't eaten anything this morning. My stomach grumbles loudly as I take a tray and load it with mashed potatoes, string beans and a slab of meat loaf.

I pass some kid selling Golly Pops, and it makes me angry that I'm not allowed to sell candy bars. He's trying to earn a trip to Hershey, and I'm trying to save our apartment. It's not fair!

Back at our table, I let out a breath and nod as Toothpick passes me a corn muffin from his lunch. It's moist and delicious. For some reason, watching Toothpick chow down on a thermos full of warm chili and a bag of clementine slices that his dad prepared makes me miss my dad.

To keep from getting teary, I pull out my Royal-T slogans and get to work. "Superior for your posterior." I tap my pen on the table. "Pamper your superior rear-e-or. Your superior posterior. Pamper your . . ." It makes me feel better to work on them and imagine winning the grand prize.

Toothpick pulls a movie makeup magazine from his backpack.

"The best thing for your posterior, your rear-e-or, is Royal-T, I swear-e-or."

"That's so cool," Toothpick says, and I think he's talking about my slogan until he shoves a photo in my face of what appears to be a jawless zombie. "I could totally do that with the right supplies."

"Totally," I say, but I'm not really paying attention. Jawless zombies are fun, but they're not going to win me ten thousand dollars in the Royal-T contest. Giving my slogan extra pizzazz will. And I have a real chance to win, because it's a skill contest—coming up with a clever slogan in twenty-five words or fewer—and most people don't bother entering contests that require a skill.

"I'm going to win the ten grand," I tell Toothpick. "I just need a little something extra to make my slogan stand out."

Toothpick looks at me and says, "You'll figure it out." Then he says, "It will be amazing when you win."

This time I know he's talking about me, and it makes me feel great.

Dear Benjamin Epstein,

Thank you for your recent letter.

I wish we had a job for someone of your talents, but all the employees at Royal-T Bathroom Tissue Company are at least eighteen years old.

I sincerely hope you and your mother find a solution to your problem.

Enclosed please find a coupon for a complimentary package of four rolls of Royal-T Bathroom Tissue.

Regards,
Ed Chase
Community Relations Representative,
  Royal-T Bathroom Tissue Company

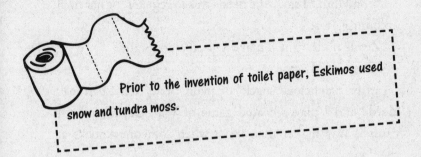

Prior to the invention of toilet paper, Eskimos used snow and tundra moss.

After school, I find a letter from Ed Chase in our mailbox. He enclosed another coupon for a free four-pack of toilet paper. *Note to self: Continue correspondence with Royal-T. The free toilet paper is definitely worth the price of the stamps. Besides, I like getting the letters.*

There's also an envelope from the National Association of State Boards of Accountancy in our mailbox.

I put it on the table so Mom will see it when she comes home. The envelope makes me feel like we're moving in the right direction, toward Dad's Grand Plan, even though I'm still worried about Mr. Katz's threat of eviction. I could tell he was serious, and that would blow apart Dad's Grand Plan for us.

Zeyde asks, "What's that? Something good?"

"For Mom," I say. "She needs this to register for her final accounting test."

Zeyde nods. "She'll make a good accountant."

"She will," I agree.

After a delicious snack* of plain Boaty Oats oatmeal, Zeyde and I play a heated game of War. Zeyde's pile of cards is way higher than mine when someone knocks at the door.

Zeyde tilts his head. *"Nu?"*

"I'll get it," I say.

Zeyde stays at the table, tapping his hefty deck of cards with his too-long fingernails.

This time, I remember to ask who it is, but I'm sorry I do.

"Mr. Katz."

I open the door, feeling like I'm inviting the grim reaper into our apartment. "Hello." I swallow past my tight throat.

Mr. Katz taps his foot. I can tell his shoes are the expensive kind—the kind people wear at funerals. "Is your mother here?" He looks past me and waves at Zeyde.

"Hello," Zeyde says, shuffling his cards. "I'm going to get some crackers to munch on till your mom comes home with dinner."

"They're in the cabinet," I say to Zeyde, then turn to Mr.

_____

*A fine example of my Sultan of Sarcasm skills (and nice alliteration, too).

Katz. "She's still at work," I say quietly, even though I know that's a lie. She's studying at the library to prepare for the CPA exam. Her work closes at three o'clock, which was a couple hours ago.

Mr. Katz bites his bottom lip, like he's thinking about something. Then he pulls a bright orange piece of paper from his briefcase. He peels off the backing and presses it onto our front door—right next to where I'm standing.

"I'm really sorry, Ben," he mutters, then jogs down the steps and leaves.

I'm standing there looking at a bright orange eviction notice. TEN DAYS TO PAY, it says in bold letters.

Terrific!

I know exactly what happens if Mom can't pay in ten days, because I read about it at the library. Mr. Katz will file a motion—whatever that means!—to take Mom to court, like she's some kind of criminal. By then, we'll owe a total of $2,650.

Maybe with Mom's salary and tips, the social security benefit of $600 for me we get each month, and help from Zeyde, we'll be able to pay in time. Maybe.

I pick at the corner of the notice, trying to get it off so Mom doesn't see it when she comes home, but the entire thing is stuck on there pretty good, and I can tell it's going to make a big mess if I keep picking.

When Mrs. Schneckle's door opens across the hall, I hurry inside and shut and lock our door, leaning my back against it, breathing like I just ran a mile in PE.

I squeeze my eyelids closed and hear Mrs. Schneckle's footsteps, then her breathing on the other side of our door. Heat races through my cheeks. I can't stand that she's reading that notice. Everyone from the upper apartments will see it, too, when they walk by, and any visitors who come in. Mr. Katz might as well have tacked up a flashing neon sign: THE EPSTEINS ARE LOSERS WHO CAN'T PAY THEIR RENT!

Dad would have hated that notice on our door. *Hated it!*

"That Mr. Katz is a *shmendrik*," Mrs. Schneckle mutters.

I have to bite my lip to keep from laughing on my side of the door.

"A big *s–h–m–e–n–d–r–i–k*!"

When I hear her footsteps recede, then the downstairs door creak open and closed, my shoulders relax.

"Boychik, come here," Zeyde says.

I startle and look over.

Zeyde's patting my chair.

He was so quiet, I'd forgotten he was sitting at the table.

"Who was that nice man?" Zeyde asks. "A salesman?"

A salesman? I can't tell Zeyde the truth. He'll feel even worse about moving in with us. Maybe Mom can figure out how to get that notice off the door before Zeyde sees it. "No one, Zeyde," I say. "Mind if we play cards later? I forgot about some homework I have to do."

"Of course," Zeyde says, gathering all the cards into one deck, but his eyes look sad.

I hurry into my bedroom, feeling bad for deserting

Zeyde, but I'm not up for cards. I slide under my comforter, appreciating that it smells like laundry soap now instead of pizza vomit. I feel ashamed to look up at the galaxy, but I do anyway. "What am I supposed to do?"

Of course my ceiling is silent, as ceilings are.

"I'm trying to stick with the Grand Plan," I say to him. "Tell me what else I can do."

Tears attempt to muscle their way out of my eyes. Some succeed and dribble down my cheeks. I brush away the wetness and go into Mom's room.

It's quiet in there, and everything's organized. Mom's bed is carefully made, with a blue smiley-face pillow leaning against the headboard. Her books are in two crates along the wall, sorted from smallest to tallest. There are no clothes sticking out of her closet or drawers. Even the small table near her bed is clear of papers and junk and has only a framed photo and a small pencil holder with three pens in it, capped and leaning in the same direction.

Mom is so neat and precise she *needs* to be an accountant. She was made for the job, not to serve greasy bacon strips, endless cups of coffee and stacks of pancakes to inconsiderate people who sometimes leave lousy tips in puddles of syrup.

The framed photo next to Mom's bed is one of Dad. I hold it, push my glasses up on my nose and examine the image of my father. He's standing on a beach, probably in Florida, wearing swim trunks and pretending he's Mr. Universe or something, flexing his biceps. I flex my own

— 93 —

right biceps, but nothing much changes. Same with my left. "Someday."

I take a deep breath but can't steady my insides.

The memories are too much. I put down the picture of Dad, grab my jacket from my room and tell Zeyde, "I'm going out for a little while."

"I thought you had homework to do," Zeyde says.

"I'm doing it at my friend's house," I say, even though he must know I'm lying, because my backpack is on the couch, right where I left it when I came home from school.

"Have fun," he says, absently shuffling the cards we were playing with.

"I will," I say, even though it's weird to tell someone to have fun after they say they're doing homework, even when they're lying.

When I step out of our apartment, a weight lifts off me. The weight of memories. I actually feel physically lighter until I close our door and see the bright orange paper plastered to it, with two words in bold letters: EVICTION NOTICE.

Terrific!

I rocket out of the apartment building into the cool air and kick through crispy leaves all the way to Toothpick's house.

Mr. Taylor opens the door, and I'm hit with a wave of delicious smells.

"Just in time," he says, looking genuinely happy to see me. "Since I'm off tonight, I made veggie stew with homemade biscuits." He pulls me inside by the elbow. "Go up to Michael's room, and I'll call you guys when dinner's ready."

It sounds weird to hear Toothpick called Michael, even though I know that's his real name. I've just been calling him Toothpick for so long.

"Thanks, Mr. Taylor." I unzip my jacket and jog upstairs.

In Toothpick's room, Psycho rubs against my ankles, which makes me feel welcomed. Pick shows me some new scar wax he bought and pictures of what he can make with it.

"Gross," I say.

"Right?" he says, super excited.

I never saw anyone so jazzed about creating fake bodily injuries.

"Want me to give you a neck wound?" he asks.

I rub my neck. "No, I'm good. Thanks."

"Come on," Pick whines. "I can make it look like a nail is coming out of it. Imagine your mom's face when she sees that!"

I wish Toothpick hadn't said that, because I imagine Mom's face, but not her seeing some dumb fake neck wound. I imagine her seeing that lousy bright orange notice plastered to our front door when she comes home from studying at the library. I imagine her sinking down in her chair at the table and putting her head in her hands. I imagine her throwing out the letter she got today from the National Association of State Boards of Accountancy and taking the $190.35 Grand Plan money and giving it to that *shmendrik* Mr. Katz, all while wearing her stupid paper piggy hat.

I came to Toothpick's house to get away from everything, but "everything," it seems, followed me here. "I've got to go," I tell Toothpick. "I need to get home."

Toothpick reels back like I hit him. "But you just got here. I have a bunch of cool stuff I want to show you."

I take a deep whiff of the rich smells of stew and biscuits. "I know," I say, wishing I'd never come over in the first place. "But I forgot something important I have to do at home." That's almost true.

"Can't you do it later?" Pick holds up the scar wax. "Let me give you at least one cool scar."

"Sorry, Pick. Next time."

I pet Psycho behind the ears and leave without saying good-bye to Mr. Taylor.

The whole walk home through the annoying crunching leaves and chilly air, I think that I don't need Toothpick to give me a scar on the outside.

I've got a really big one on the inside that apparently no one but me knows is there.

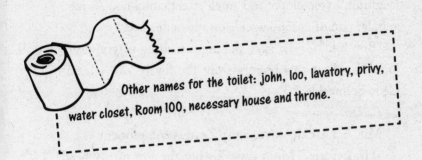

Other names for the toilet: john, loo, lavatory, privy, water closet, Room 100, necessary house and throne.

When I walk into the foyer, I touch Dad's name on our mailbox out of habit. I avert my eyes from the notice as I put my key in the lock of our apartment door, but it's hard, because the notice is so bright.

Sounds come from inside the apartment that I'm sure are crying.

Terrific!

I consider whirling around and going back to Toothpick's house. I could tell him I finished what I needed to; then I'd enjoy a meal of stew and biscuits, get a fake scar on my neck and have a cat rub against my ankles . . . or I could go inside and deal with Mom crying her eyeballs out.

I open our apartment door.

Mom, Zeyde and Mrs. Schneckle are near the table—laughing. I step closer and smell sweet cinnamon. A rectangular pan of peach kugel is on the table. *Score!*

"Boychik!" Zeyde says, pulling me into a playful headlock. "Look at this bounty from the lovely and talented Celia Schneckle."

Celia?

Mrs. Schneckle waves away Zeyde's compliment.

"Hi, sweetie," Mom says, kissing the top of my head. "Mrs. Schneckle brought over dinner. Wasn't that nice?"

No one has mentioned the eviction notice plastered on our door.

"I'm tired of eating by myself," Mrs. Schneckle says. "Since Marvin died, dinnertime is the worst."

My stomach twists. I didn't know Mrs. Schneckle even had a husband. He must have died a long time ago, because I don't remember him at all.

Mom puts an arm around Mrs. Schneckle's shoulders. "You can join us anytime. Next time I'll cook."

"That would be lovely," Mrs. Schneckle says, leaning her head toward Mom's.

I can't imagine what Mom would make for dinner. I don't think Mrs. Schneckle would like pancakes, plain oatmeal or cheese and crackers.

"Come on," Zeyde says, pushing me into a chair and handing me an empty plate. "Serve yourself that good kugel before it gets cold." Zeyde takes another plate. "Or before I eat it all."

Mom's sitting in her seat, eyes closed, inhaling the scent of warm, sweet kugel.

"Thanks," I say to Mrs. Schneckle, and mean it. And not only for the food. I'm pretty sure Mrs. Schneckle is the reason Mom looks so happy, despite the eviction notice on our door.

Zeyde pulls out a chair for Mrs. Schneckle. Dad's chair—the one Zeyde's been sitting in. "For you, Celia."

"Oh, I'm going back to my apartment," Mrs. Schneckle says, her cheeks reddening.

I realize there are four of us and only three chairs. I grab my plate and stand. "Sit here, Mrs. Schneckle. I like to stand while I eat." *That sounded dumb. Who likes to stand while they eat?*

"Oh, no," she says. "I've got to get back."

Zeyde hands Mrs. Schneckle a plate piled with kugel and salad. Then he takes his own loaded plate, loops his arm around her elbow and says, "May I?"

Zeyde's such a dork.

Mrs. Schneckle's cheeks redden again. "Why, I'd love your company, Jake."

Jake?

His bald head seems pinker than usual.

Mom and I watch Mrs. Schneckle and Zeyde leave, and I'm struck by how much Mrs. Schneckle reminds me of Bubbe Mary. Not how she looked but how she acted. They walk right past the bright orange eviction notice on the door.

Mom shakes her head. "Your *zeyde*'s really something." Then she pulls out an envelope. "It's here," she says. "It came today."

Still not talking about the eviction notice on the door.

"I know," I say, shoveling forkfuls of sweet, warm peach kugel into my mouth. Mrs. Schneckle put raisins in this time. I love raisins. "I brought it in from the mailbox."

"Of course," Mom says.

With Zeyde over at Mrs. Schneckle's apartment, Dad's kitchen chair is empty again, and I can't help but think how much he'd enjoy eating the kugel, how much we'd enjoy having him here again. Just the three of us.

"I'm doing it," Mom says, waving the envelope. "It's the invitation to register for the fourth and final test." Mom puts her hand on mine and squeezes. "I'm going to register at the library tomorrow and put the money in the mail. I can't believe they make you pay a registration fee of ninety-five dollars *plus* an examination fee of one ninety thirty-five. But what can you do?"

I want to ask Mom if she saw the notice outside our door, because it's weird she hasn't said anything. I want to ask how she's comfortable with spending $190.35 to register for the test when we can't pay the rent.

"I don't know what's going to happen, Benjamin," Mom says. "But I've got to do this one thing. Your dad worked that extra shift at the *Inquirer* so I could finish my courses. And he earned extra money painting houses instead of canvases, like he'd wanted to, so I could take the other three tests. When he got sick, I had only the last of the four tests to take before I could get my license. He so wanted this for us, Ben. It's taken me a while to get back on my feet and start studying again, but I've got to take and pass that last test. For him." Mom squeezes my wrist. "For us."

Thank you, Dad.

"Despite that awful notice plastered on our door for everyone to see!"

She saw it.

Mom's cheeks get pink.

"But how are we—"

"I don't want to think about it right now," Mom says. "I just want to enjoy this delicious dinner from Mrs. Schneckle. All right?"

"Sure."

Mom slips a forkful of kugel into her mouth and closes her eyelids.

The look on her face—pure bliss—makes everything feel okay, even though Dad's chair is still empty and the eviction notice is still plastered to our door.

• • •

Later, I'm working on my Royal-T slogan at the table and Mom's studying her accounting textbook when Zeyde returns.

"That Celia is a class act," he says. "You should see the toilet paper she has over there. I used it to blow my *shnoz*."

Zeyde kisses his fingertips and releases them skyward. "Good stuff! Just like the stuff you gave me the other day, Ben."

Dork-o-rama!

"Did you have a nice time?" Mom asks, looking up from her book.

Zeyde rubs his belly. "Delicious!"

Mom smiles.

"Now, if you'll excuse me," Zeyde says, "I need to retire to the throne for a few minutes."

Zeyde heads down the hallway, and I look at Mom.

She leans close and whispers, "'Throne' is a fancy word for 'toilet.'"

"Really?" Tiny fireworks explode in my brain, and I tap my paper with the pencil. "People really say 'throne' instead of 'toilet'? You're serious?"

"Of course I'm serious."

"YES!"

Mom looks at me like I'm crazy, but I don't care, because now—NOW!—I have that certain something that will make my slogan the one that wins the ten thousand dollars. *Thank you, Zeyde!*

I neatly print my new and improved slogan. Then I put it in an envelope and kiss it for good luck, like I do every time I send off an important sweepstakes entry.

"Yes!" I say again, leaning back, feeling like a weight's been lifted off me.

"Good luck," Mom says. "I hope you win the big one this time."

"Me too," I say. *I just hope the prize money comes in time.*

Zeyde's in the bathroom again later when I climb into bed. He's probably putting his teeth in a glass on the sink. At least, I hope so!

I figure if I can fall asleep before Zeyde starts snoring, I have a chance of sleeping through it. But if he snores first, it'll be impossible to fall asleep.

As I lie there watching Barkley dart through his castle, I'm glad Mom's moving forward with the Grand Plan by registering for the test tomorrow, despite everything that's going on. And I'm so happy Zeyde gave me the word that provided my entry with that certain zing that might make it stand out from the rest.

In the cafeteria at our lunch table, Toothpick munches on a chocolate-covered biscotti and passes me one. When I take it, I notice a small pencil plunged into the back of his hand.

"Oh my . . . !" *Who did that? Angus Andrews?*

A smile spreads across Toothpick's face.

I'm sure his grin is caused by the raging infection from his hand that must have spread to his brain. "Seriously, Pick!"

Toothpick cracks up, and I can see chewed-up biscotti on his tongue. "Great, right? I totally got you."

I look closely at the bluish-red swelling around the pencil, which is clearly jammed into the back of his hand. "That's not a pencil?"

"No, it's a pencil. Moron."

A guy at the far end of our table looks over at us like we're weird.

Toothpick makes a face at him, then leans in toward me. "Scar wax."

"It looks real," I say. "It looks . . . infected, dude."

The guy at the end of our table looks at us like we're making him sick.

Toothpick glares, then opens his mouth with the chewed-up biscotti.

"Ew," I say, but at least it makes the guy turn away from us.

Toothpick shows me a magazine with a picture of a hand that looks just like his. "Besides the scar wax, it's a little fake blood and reddish-brown powder and—"

Toothpick gets as excited about movie makeup artistry as I get about sweepstakes and contests. I wonder if Pick kisses his hand when he makes a particularly wicked-looking wound, like I kiss my sweepstakes envelopes for good luck before I send them off. *Maybe we are weird.*

"Hi, losers," Delaney says as she walks by our table with her box of lousy Golly Pops.

"I can't stand that girl," I say, crunching into my biscotti.

"But she's totally cute," Toothpick says.

"Totally," I admit.

Toothpick gives me a fist bump with his "wounded" hand. "Hey, want to come over after school?"

I think of returning home to the bright orange eviction

notice on our door. I think of Mom sometimes accidentally wearing her paper piggy hat when she comes home from work and studying, and I think of Zeyde being with it sometimes and so confused other times.

"Definitely," I say.

• • •

At Toothpick's, it's just Psycho and us, because his dad's at work. Toothpick's mom moved out a long time ago.

She used to bake delicious cakes and cookies for us and once helped us build a fort from blankets and sheets in their living room. When we were done, the three of us hung out in the fort, eating warm slices of banana bread while his mom held a flashlight and read to us from *Charlotte's Web*. She read to us like that every day for two weeks. At the end of *Charlotte's Web*, when the sad thing happened, Toothpick and I both cried.

We were little then.

Toothpick visits his mom for a week in the summer and over winter break. He doesn't talk about her much, other than to say she doesn't let him watch horror movies when he's there, which is kind of stupid because Pick *is* horror movies. He says she doesn't realize he's not a little kid anymore, which is kind of dumb because Pick is as tall as a grown man, even though he's only in seventh grade. Mrs. Taylor's tall, too. Really tall. Pick told me she played basketball on her high school team.

In his room, Toothpick changes into shorts and creates a wound on his knee with a nail stuck in it. It's pretty cool how he spreads the scar wax, makes an indentation and fills it with fake blood, then spreads powder around the edges to make it look gross and infected.

But after Toothpick creates his third wound, I get bored and look around the Internet on his computer. I find a few new mail-in sweepstakes and write down the information so I can enter them later at home. One of the sweepstakes is giving away a video camera, which I would totally give to Toothpick, if he didn't already have a really nice one his dad gave him a couple years ago for his birthday. If I won, I'd probably sell the camera and give the money to Mom.

I also check out Toothpick's YouTube channel. He's got his three short horror films posted there. He told me he hopes a producer stumbles across it and asks him to make a movie in Hollywood.

"Hey," I say. "You got a new comment on *The Terror Train*."

"What's it say?"

"Heart it! Please make more movies!"

A grin spreads across Toothpick's face. "I should come up with my next one soon."

"Definitely. Your fans are waiting."

Toothpick laughs. "You mean my fan is waiting."

"Ha. You've got like forty comments on each of your movies. You're practically famous, dude."

"Practically."

I look around online for more contests and discover that Charmin and Cheap Chic—whatever they are—run a contest for the best wedding dress *made entirely from toilet paper*, glue, tape, needle and thread. "I could do that," I mumble.

"Hmm?" Toothpick says.

I show Toothpick the winning toilet paper wedding dress from last year, being modeled by the person who created it. "How cool is that?"

"A toilet paper dress? Weird," Toothpick says as he slathers a fake wound with fake blood.

"Yeah, like that's not weird," I say, pointing to the fake wounds all over his body.

Toothpick shrugs.

"The person who makes the best dress gets over two thousand bucks."

"Now, that's cool," Toothpick says, breaking a pencil near the eraser so he can create another fake pencil puncture wound, this time on top of his foot.

There's a video online that shows how to make a rose with a stem out of two squares of toilet paper.

I grab a long length of toilet paper from the hall bathroom and work on making roses. They're easy to do—just a few folds. When I'm finished, I have six droopy toilet paper roses.

There are sites that teach all kinds of toilet paper origami. I could make a toilet paper swan, boat or butterfly, but those things look complicated, so I don't bother.

If I could somehow make an entire wedding dress from toilet paper, I could compete to win two thousand bucks this summer, when they have the contest. I just wish summer wasn't so far away. I could use that money right now. It would be almost enough to pay our back rent and the upcoming month's rent, too. If I do enter the contest, I'll have to borrow Pick's camera and find someone willing to model my toilet paper dress for the video submission.

Toothpick's tall. It would be hilarious if he modeled the toilet paper wedding dress for the video. Humor and creativity count for a lot in these contests.

I look over at Pick. He's covered with fake wounds. I wonder what it would take to get him to agree to model a toilet paper wedding dress.

"What?" Toothpick asks, looking up at me.

I push my glasses up on my nose. "Nothing."

"Then quit staring at me. You're freaking me out."

"You're covered with fake pencil and nail wounds, and I'm freaking you out?"

"Yeah."

My stomach rumbles. "I'm starving."

"Me too. Let's go downstairs and see what my dad left for us."

In the kitchen, with Psycho crunching bits from her food bowl, Toothpick and I devour a couple slabs of cold broccoli-cheese casserole and a quart of Rita's mango ice for dessert.

It's dark when I finally head home.

The cold air feels great. I take deep breaths and wish my dad could feel this crisp air. He loved fall. Colorful leaves to crunch through. On Halloween, he wore crazy costumes to freak out the little kids in our neighborhood. And this was the season he had the Eagles on TV to scream at.

Too bad our cable got turned off when Mom couldn't pay the bill. It doesn't matter. I don't care about the Eagles anymore without Dad here.

I open the door to our apartment building and touch Dad's nameplate—TODD EPSTEIN—for luck, then check our mailbox. My shoulders slump when I find it empty. *No contest wins or free toilet paper coupons today. Not even a lousy bill.*

At our apartment door, I pull out the six paper roses from my backpack to give to Mom. Fishing for my key—in front of the eviction notice—I hear Mom screaming.

I jam my key in the lock, turn the knob and shove the door open.

Mom's at the kitchen sink, holding up a sopping roll of gray toilet paper.

Zeyde's standing near the sink, running a hand over his bald head again and again, like he's pushing back hair that isn't there.

"Dad!" Mom yells, shaking the soaking roll over the sink. "I'm going to ask you again. What were you thinking?"

"It was so rough, Shelley," Zeyde says. "I wanted to make it softer." Zeyde bites his bottom lip, and I know where

Mom gets that habit from. "I really don't know what I was thinking. I'm sorry, Shell. Please don't be mad, sweetheart. You and Ben are my favorite Philadelphians. Remember?"

Mom lets out a long, defeated breath. "Oh, Dad." Then she turns to me. "Hi, honey."

I hand Mom the bouquet of toilet paper roses, hoping it will make her happier.

She looks at the roses and tilts her head. "Toilet paper roses, huh?" An odd sound comes from her throat, and I'm not sure if it's crying or laughter. "Appropriate," Mom says. "*Oy vey*. How appropriate." She kisses the top of my head, then drops the saturated roll of toilet paper into the trash can. "Your *zeyde* just soaked an entire roll of toilet paper in the sink."

"Oh," I say, wondering why he'd think that would make the toilet paper softer.

"Dad," Mom says, her voice high and tight, "you left the water running in the sink. If I hadn't come home, the place could have flooded. That's the last thing we need." Mom presses the heel of her hand against her temple, like she's pushing back a headache. "I'm sorry I didn't buy new toilet paper with the money you gave me, Dad. I was waiting until we ran out of the other stuff. I didn't want to waste it."

Zeyde stands there, running his hand over his bald head, his lips moving, like he's working out a difficult problem.

I wish Zeyde would at least say something. I wish I'd have come home earlier instead of messing around at Toothpick's house, wasting time. I could have stopped

Zeyde before he even got to the sink. I could have given him a good roll of toilet paper from the stash in my closet. I could have kept this from happening.

"Soaking toilet paper doesn't make it softer," Mom says, as though she's talking to a little kid. "It ruins it. And we can't afford to waste *anything* right now."

The worry line forms between Mom's eyebrows, and I can't blame Mr. Katz this time.

"Sorry," Zeyde mutters. He reaches into his pocket. "I'll pay you for that, Shelley." But when Zeyde pulls out his money clip, there's no cash in it, which makes me feel sorry for him.

I can almost hear Dad telling me I need to do something to fix this situation.

I run to my room and come back with a roll of Royal-T from my closet. "Here." I give the roll to Zeyde. "Nice and soft."

Zeyde's eyes get misty. "Thank you, boychik." Zeyde presses his dry palm against my cheek, then shuffles down the hall.

When Zeyde is out of earshot, I whisper, "Mom, what's going on?"

"What's going on"—Mom collapses onto a chair—"is I'm worried about your *zeyde*." She gnaws on a thumbnail.

I sink onto my chair and remember the other night when Zeyde called me Mary. "I'm worried, too."

"Aunt Abby was looking for a place for Zeyde to live. A place with a memory-care unit. That's why he moved down there, so he'd have someplace safe to live if things got worse. I checked out places around here, but they're way overpriced."

"What are we going to do?" I ask. "Send him back to Florida?"

"I'll figure something out," Mom says.

"*We'll* figure something out," I say, getting up and making a small amendment to our Grand Plan. I add the words "and Zeyde" to the fourth point, after "Benjamin and Mom" and before "will have a better life."

Mom stands behind me, reads what I wrote out loud and squeezes my shoulder. "Have I told you lately that I love you?"

I duck my head.

Mom holds up her droopy toilet paper rose bouquet. "All I need is a cardboard toilet paper roll vase to hold them."

"I think there's one in the trash. But it might be a little wet."

"Ha ha," Mom says, but she's not really laughing.

I shrug.

"Hey. On the bright side, I signed up for the fourth and final test. Can I get a 'Woot! Woot!' people?"

Since I'm the only "people" in the room, I give Mom a seriously loud "Woot! Woot!" "When's the test?"

"October seventeenth."

That's nearly three weeks from now. I wish it were sooner but try to look on the bright side, like Dad would have done. "That gives you another two and a half weeks to study." I give Mom a fist bump, almost expecting her to have a pencil plunged into a wound on the back of her hand. But she just has a few freckles there, like I do. Then my stomach gnaws a little, because I wonder where we'll be living October 17. I push the thought out of my mind.

"And we'll get the test results a week or two later."

"That sounds good," I say, but think that November's rent will be just about due by then . . . if we even make it that long.

Zeyde comes in and puts a check on the table.

I can see from Zeyde's eyes that he's thinking more clearly now.

"What's this for, Dad?" Mom asks.

Zeyde points his thumb toward our front door. "I saw the notice on the door. I'm not blind, you know."

"I know," Mom says quietly, not touching the check.

I crane my neck and see the check's for $300. I do some quick mental math and realize Zeyde's contribution will bring the $2,650 we'll owe on October 1 down to $2,350. And when the $600 social security check arrives, it will be down to $1,750. I wish Mom could spend all her salary and tips on rent, but I know she has other bills to pay, like electric, food and Dad's medical bills. Still.

"Take it, Shelley," Zeyde says. "It's all I have right now, because that plane ticket here was so expensive. Last minute and all. And I gave Abby quite a bit of money last week to pay for a major car repair. But when I get my next monthly check and pay off my credit card, I'll be able to give you more."

I feel a wave of relief. I don't know if it will be enough, but I'm so glad Zeyde can help.

"Thank you, Dad." Mom looks like she's going to cry, or maybe she's just tired.

Zeyde nods once at Mom and once at me, then walks toward the bedroom.

Mom bites her bottom lip, takes the check, kisses the top of my head and walks toward her bedroom.

That's when I make a decision. I'm going to spend the fifty dollars in my underwear drawer. I'm going to buy more candy bars. And I'm going to sell them at school.

No matter what Mr. Sheffield said.

I've got to help Mom, too.

I promised.

In 2001, the first World Toilet Summit was held in Singapore.

The next week goes by too fast.

I don't want October eighth to arrive. That's when, according to the eviction notice, Mom has to pay all our back rent and the current rent . . . or else.

At the library, I enter as many online contests as I can. I even enter a couple mail-in contests, with prizes that make it worth using the stamps.

Unfortunately, even though I touch Dad's nameplate on the mailbox every day for luck, I don't win anything. Not even a small win, like a baseball cap or a coupon for something at the market.

On the bright side, Mrs. Schneckle makes us dinner

three times during the week. And there are enough left-overs for the other days.

Zeyde has good days and bad days. I play War with him and talk with him about some of the fun stuff we used to do together, because I think it will help his brain work better at remembering things. At least, I hope so.

Mom looks really tired every day when she comes home from work and studying, but the rent envelope is filling up with her daily tips and biweekly salary, and that's a good thing.

Except it makes me feel guilty, because the one thing I do not do all week is sell candy bars.

Every day I come up with a different excuse: woke too late to buy the candy at WaWa, legs too tired from running in PE the day before to carry an extra-heavy backpack, etc.

The truth is, I'm too scared of getting in trouble to start selling them again.

It feels like we're right near the Grand Plan finish line and I'm letting everyone down.

Especially Dad.

Dear Benjamin Epstein,

Thank you for writing to us about your grandfather. We're glad to hear he likes our bathroom tissue.

We're enclosing a coupon for a four-pack of Royal-T Bathroom Tissue to show our appreciation for your Loyal-T to Royal-T.

Regards,
Ed Chase
Community Relations Representative,
   Royal-T Bathroom Tissue Company

P.S. Q: How do you communicate with a fish?
   A: Drop it a line.

Modern Toilet is a bathroom-themed restaurant chain based in Taiwan. Patrons are seated on actual, nonworking toilets. Food is served on plastic mini toilet bowls, and drinks arrive in mini urinals, which customers can take home as souvenirs.

Today's the day—Thursday, October 8—when Mr. Katz will come to collect all the money we owe. Mom's close. We talked about it last night. With the money from Zeyde, the social security money and her work money, we only need five hundred dollars more.

Turns out Zeyde didn't have much left over to give Mom after paying his credit card bill, but he promised her more money in November.

We can't wait that long.

Mr. Katz will be here any minute.

I should have sold candy bars. It still might not have been enough, but it would have gotten us closer.

At the mailbox, I touch Dad's nameplate and pray there's

something good inside that might change everything—a five-hundred-dollar contest win, for example. There is something good: another letter from Royal-T, about Zeyde, and a coupon for a free four-pack of their toilet paper, and a dumb fish joke, which actually makes me feel a little better.

Mrs. Schneckle comes downstairs to the foyer. "Anything good, *bubeleh*?" she asks, hoisting an overstuffed pocketbook onto her shoulder.

"Just another free four-pack of toilet paper."

She pinches my cheek. "You're so talented, *bubeleh*!" Then a worried look crosses her face. "How's your *zeyde* doing?"

Did Mom tell her about the toilet paper soaking incident? "He's okay," I say, but he's really not. He's been repeating things and forgetting things. The other day he called me Barkley and didn't know who the real Barkley was when I tried to explain. And other times he's great—making sense and cracking jokes—and I think everything's going to be fine.

"That's good to hear. I worry about him sometimes."

I nod. *Me too.*

"Well, I'm off to run the Wii Bowling competition today."

I tilt my head.

"At the Jewish senior center. I run the Wii Bowling and some other activities for the residents there."

"Oh." I never thought of Mrs. Schneckle as having a job. That sounds like a fun one. "Have a good time."

"Always do." Mrs. Schneckle pats my cheek and heads outside.

Along the bottom edge of the orange eviction notice on our door, someone has written in tiny block letters: MR. KATZ IS A SHMENDRIK.

I wonder how long that's been there and who wrote it. Then I know. "Mrs. Schneckle?" I shake my head. "You totally rock!"

Inside the apartment, Zeyde's at the kitchen table, staring off at nothing. There's sweat on his bald head, and he wipes it off with a hankie. "I'm fine," he says, even though I didn't ask. "How was your day, boychik?"

"Okay," I say, not mentioning that today's the day Mr. Katz returns. Not mentioning that I was too much of a wimp to sell the candy bars. I throw my backpack on the couch, sit next to Zeyde at the table and pat his veiny hand. "Want to play War?"

"What?"

"War?"

"What's that?"

My heart skips a beat. "It's a card game," I say, wondering if he's putting me on or if his memory has gotten that bad. What I don't add is we've played it together since I was little.

"All right," he says, putting his palms on the table. "You'll teach me how to play."

"Um, okay," I say, taking off my jacket. "It goes like this. . . ." And I teach Zeyde how to play a game he taught me how to play a long time ago.

Zeyde keeps messing up, though—taking the cards when he's not supposed to—and I'm relieved when Mom comes in.

She whips off her paper piggy hat. "Not again," she says, shoving it into her pocket.

I walk over and give her a hug. She smells like bacon.

"What was that for?"

"I'm glad you're home."

Mom looks over at Zeyde. "Everything okay?"

"Definitely," I say. "We were just playing War."

"All right," she says, looking suspicious.

"It's a fun game, Shell. You should try it sometime," Zeyde says.

"I'm sure it is," Mom says.

I don't tell Mom Zeyde didn't even remember what the game was. She has enough to worry about today.

Before Mom even has her coat unbuttoned, someone knocks at the door and my heart seizes.

Zeyde walks toward the door. "I'll get it."

Mom puts a hand on his arm. "I've got it, Dad."

And she slips outside to deal with Mr. Katz privately.

"Come on," I say to Zeyde. "I know another card game."

"What's it called?" Zeyde asks.

"War," I say, joking.

"Oh, I don't know that one."

I don't think he's joking, and it makes me so sad I can't even shuffle the cards.

Zeyde and I wait, the deck of cards lying on the table between us.

Mom comes back in, goes to her room, returns with an envelope, hands something to Mr. Katz and closes the door.

Then she nods and walks back toward her room.

"Excuse me, Zeyde," I say.

I catch up with Mom at her bedroom door. "So?"

We go into my room and sit on my bed.

"It's done, Ben."

I look up at the stars, then at Mom. "What's done?"

Mom takes a breath before answering. "Mr. Katz said he's going to file papers with the court."

"But we only owe him five hundred dollars." Mrs. Schneckle is right. He is a *shmendrik*.

"Oh, Ben, I don't think it's Mr. Katz. He's a decent enough guy. He let us slide for a while. His partner is bearing down on him, not letting him give us any more time."

I bite my thumbnail. "If Mr. Katz is going to file papers with the court, that actually buys us a little more time. I looked it up in the library. Now you have until the court date to pay everything we owe."

"And if the court date is next month, we'll have to pay November's rent, too."

"Yeah, I guess so," I say.

Mom's shoulders slump. "We're so close. I'm going to take the test on the seventeenth."

"And you're going to pass."

Mom looks up at the stars on my ceiling. "With flying colors. Then a week or two later, I should have the results, then—"

"You'll get that great job at Mr. Daniels's firm," I say.

"Making more than twice what I'm making now."

"And you won't have to wear that stupid pig hat."

"Best part of all," Mom says, running a hand through her wild hair. "We just have to make it till then." Mom leans back on my bed and stares at the ceiling.

"We'll make it," I say, flopping onto my back next to Mom and looking up at Dad's universe.

I know we will, because I've decided that even if I'm scared—terrified, actually—of getting caught, I'm going to spend the fifty bucks from my underwear drawer at WaWa tomorrow.

I, Benjamin Epstein, enterprising entrepreneur, am back in the candy bar business.

Despite the common misconception, Thomas Crapper didn't invent the toilet. Crapper did have a successful plumbing career in England and held nine plumbing-related patents. But an employee of his, Albert Giblin, holds the 1819 British patent for the Silent Valveless Water Waste Preventer, which allowed a toilet to flush effectively. Crapper most likely bought the patent rights from Giblin and marketed the device himself.

The next day, I touch the fifty dollar bills that are practically exploding from my pocket and walk quickly to the closest WaWa. I can't be late for school, because I can't do anything to attract attention to myself. Not now.

The WaWa is jammed with people buying coffees, ordering breakfast sandwiches and purchasing newspapers. Seeing the *Inquirer* on the counter reminds me of Dad. I remember how cool he looked in his uniform when he worked as a security guard there.

Thinking of Dad gives me new resolve for selling the candy bars.

When it's my turn at the register, I say, "A hundred candy bars," and grab them from the boxes under the counter as fast as I can.

It feels like the people behind me in line are getting annoyed, because it takes a while to count out a hundred candy bars.

The lady rings me up and holds out her hand for payment. "Whoa. That's a lot of candy bars," she says, cracking her gum. "Stocking up early for Halloween?"

I nod, pay, grab the bags and zoom out of the store. I'll wake earlier Monday and go to the other WaWa. I don't need anyone getting suspicious about why I'm buying so many candy bars.

By the time I arrive at Remington Middle, I have a backpack full of a hundred candy bars, my books in my arms, and I'm in business.

"Why are you carrying your books?" Pick asks when he sees me in the hall.

"I'm selling candy bars again," I whisper.

"But—"

"Shh," I say.

He looks around. "Be careful, Ben."

"I will."

At lunch, I start at Trevor Duxbury and Brice Reid's table. As I hand out the candy bars and take people's money, I tell each person to keep it out of sight, but I see some people eating them right away, behind books or not even trying to hide them at all.

I hold my backpack close and look around for Mr. Sheffield.

"You sure you want to do this?" Pick asks as I sit at our table.

No, but I have to. "Yeah, it'll be fine. Don't worry."

"Here comes Delaney," Pick says, and I shove my backpack by my feet under the table.

"Thanks."

"Hi, Delaney," Toothpick says, which is weird, because he's never nice to her.

"Hi," she says, as though she's suspicious. She stops, her box of Golly Pops under her arm. "Why are you being nice?"

Pick shrugs. "'Cause I'm a nice guy."

"No you're not." She whirls around and heads off.

I don't know why, but this makes me laugh.

"I don't like that girl," he says. "Even if she is cute."

"Right," I say. "But she is. Totally adorable."

"I know," Toothpick says. "Why can't cute girls ever be nice, too?"

I shrug, thinking that would be a question I'd probably ask my dad.

"Hey," Toothpick says, "maybe you could sell your candy bars in the neighborhood instead. Door to door. Tell them it's a fund-raiser for school or something."

"That's amazing."

"What?" Toothpick asks.

"You actually had a good idea."

He kicks me under the table

I sneak candy bar sales throughout the day between classes, but I'm nervous and my stomach feels sick from worrying about getting caught.

When the day is over, I still have ten left. Not bad, but I know I could have sold more if I wasn't so worried.

I decide to try Toothpick's idea.

On my way home from school, I walk up to a house and knock on the door. A huge guy wearing a tank top answers. He smells sour, like he hasn't showered in a few days. I feel like running away but force myself to say, "Hi, I'm selling candy for school."

Slam!

I knock on the door of another house on the next block.

"Hi, I'm selling candy for school."

Growl! Bark! Bark! Bark! Snap!

Looking up at the gray, swirly clouds, I decide I can't give up.

I knock on another door, sure this will be the one. When a woman wearing curlers opens the door, I think maybe I'll get lucky and unload all ten candy bars.

"Hi, I'm—"

Slam!

I give up!

I return home with ten candy bars and vow to sell 110 candy bars at school on Monday to make up for it, but I'll have to be careful. Really careful.

Why is everything so hard?

Saturday, in his room, Toothpick and I talk about Halloween. Actually, Toothpick mostly talks.

"How about if we go as conjoined monster twins?" Toothpick asks. "We can sew the sleeves of two shirts together so it looks like we're attached. Then I can deck us out with really cool makeup. It'll be awesome."

"Sounds great," I say with zero enthusiasm, because I'm thinking about last Halloween.

"What?" Pick asks, kicking my sneaker and twirling around in his chair.

"Nothing." Dad was so sick last Halloween that I didn't go trick-or-treating.

"What?" Toothpick stands and pushes his chair under the desk. "We have to go trick-or-treating before we get too old. I'll make a really cool costume for us. You have to!"

I don't say anything.

"I mean, you didn't go last year."

We're both silent, until I say I have to leave.

Sunday I call Toothpick and tell him I'm sorry, that his conjoined-monster-twin costume idea is great. I guess I don't sound convincing, because Toothpick says he has to help his dad with something and hangs up. He's probably still annoyed that I'm not as excited as he is about going out trick-or-treating. I can't help how I feel. Halloween brings up difficult memories for me—how much Dad loved the holiday and how sick he was this time last year.

Zeyde reads and naps most of the day.

After her shift at work, Mom studies.

I try to do homework, but mostly I think about Dad and wish he were still here.

I'm so bummed I can't even muster the energy to pull out my *Sweeps-a-Lot* newsletter and enter a few contests. I eat one of my leftover candy bars and feel guilty about it. Even Barkley looks at me like I did something wrong.

"It's only one candy bar," I tell Barkley.

"Huh?"

For a moment, I think Barkley answered me, but then I realize it was only Zeyde, who I thought was napping. "Nothing, Zeyde," I say. "Go back to sleep."

"Okay, Mary."

Terrific!

The only good thing about the whole weekend is Mrs. Schneckle comes over Sunday evening with a pot of warm vegetable soup and homemade sourdough bread that's delicious.

Monday, October 12, Pick's waiting at my locker. He gives me a fist bump, and I know everything is okay between us. Too bad I'm so worried about selling 110 candy bars today (minus the one I ate over the weekend). I wish this stupid month was over and Mom was working as an accountant and I didn't have to sell these things anymore. I wish the Grand Plan was already in place. But at least I'm stashing the candy bar money in my underwear drawer, so

I'll be able to give Mom a big pile of cash when she'll need it most.

Still, I think Delaney will show up and scream, "Caught you!" or Mr. Sheffield will put his abnormally large hand on my shoulder and drag me to his office to call Mom and suspend me. I tell all my customers they have to keep it on the down low, but I know it takes only one person, one mistake, to get me in a world of trouble.

I sell all 109 candy bars by the end of the school day, and it does feel good to have money in my backpack again. I can't wait to add it to the money in my secret stash in the underwear drawer.

Tuesday, October 13, I return to school with another hundred candy bars, ready to do battle. I feel a great sense of relief the moment I sell the last one. Kids are coming up to me now, and it's going more quickly. I can't believe I haven't gotten caught. Maybe this will work out after all. Maybe dumb Angus Andrews isn't so dumb—just smelly. Maybe Mr. Sheffield won't do anything to me after all.

Wednesday, Delaney Phillips is absent, so I don't have to be quite as careful. I manage to sell out before lunch is over.

"Thanks, Dad," I whisper, because I'm sure he has something to do with me selling the candy bars and not getting caught. Somehow he's enabling me to help Mom stick with the Grand Plan.

In two days, on Friday, October 16, when school lets

out, I plan to hand Mom all the money I've made. I'm sure that when she adds my money with the money she's made from working, we'll be able to pay Mr. Katz the five hundred dollars we owe. Then Mom won't even have to go to court.

Maybe we'll actually have enough money left over to celebrate at the Country Club Diner again.

In the locker room on Wednesday, Angus Andrews asks if I have any candy bars left.

"Nope," I say. "Sold them all." But inside, I'm thinking, *Please don't tell. Please don't tell.*

"Cool," Angus says. "Make sure you have some tomorrow. I'll buy 'em from you."

"Okay," I say, but I'm worried about having anything to do with Angus Andrews.

But I guess there's no harm in taking the guy's money.

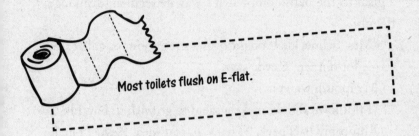

Most toilets flush on E-flat.

After school, I touch Dad's nameplate and check the mail, hoping for a contest win.

The only thing in the mailbox is an envelope from the Common Pleas Court of Philadelphia.

Gulp. Mr. Katz kept his rotten promise.

I consider throwing the envelope away but know I can't do that. I think of hiding it but won't do that either.

Inside our apartment, I put the envelope on the table, where Zeyde's reading a thick book.

He slams it shut when he sees me. "That Styron is a great writer," Zeyde says, tapping the cover. "I think I read this before but can't remember, so it's new to me." Zeyde gives me a big smile with his fake white teeth.

I still get grossed out every morning when I see them in a glass in the bathroom, but it's way better than drinking them!

"Mrs. Schneckle brought over a mushroom noodle casserole for dinner," Zeyde says.

My mouth waters.

"I think we should make a salad to go with it, boychik."

I drop my backpack. "That's a great idea, Zeyde, but I don't think we have anything to make salad with."

Zeyde waves a twenty-dollar bill. "Your mom left this for us to get some food."

I walk with Zeyde all the way to the ACME supermarket to pick up lettuce, carrots and tomatoes. We also have enough money to buy a melon and a couple frozen pizzas for tomorrow's dinner.

When Zeyde jokes around with our cashier, I know he's having a good day.

Inside the foyer of our apartment, Mrs. Schneckle's at her mailbox.

"Another junk-mail day," she says, waving a couple envelopes. "Why can't they put something good in my mailbox, like George Clooney?"

Zeyde laughs.

Old-people humor.

"At least it was a good day at the center," she says. "They had a woman come in and sing the oldies. Everyone was in such a good mood, there wasn't a single argument all day. Maybe you'd like to come there sometime, Jake."

Zeyde waves a hand dismissively. "Eh, that's for old people."

Mrs. Schneckle shrugs. "It's fun."

"Yeah, it's fun," I say, even though I have no idea what it is.

"You gentlemen take care of each other."

"Will do," I say, slinging my arm around Zeyde's back. "And thanks for the casserole, Mrs. Schneckle. It looks delicious."

"It was one of Marvin's favorites," she says, then shakes her head. "You guys enjoy it. I need to go sew a couple beanbags for a game they're playing at the center tomorrow."

When we get inside our apartment, Mom's already there, her head in her hands.

I see that the envelope on the table has been opened, so I go over and touch Mom's shoulder.

She jerks up. Her eyes are red-rimmed. "November second," she says.

"What?" I sit beside her while Zeyde puts away our groceries.

Mom pushes curls off her forehead and smoothes out the letter.

After Zeyde puts away the food, he comes over, kisses Mom's cheek, takes his book and heads down the hallway. "I'll be back in a few minutes."

Mom leans close and whispers, "The court date is November second."

"We'll have enough by then," I say, knowing that

between my candy bar money and Mom's pay and tips, we'll have that five hundred dollars paid well before the end of the month.

Mom leans her forehead into mine and makes a noise like a hiccup. "I got laid off."

I pull back, feeling like I was punched in the gut. "What?"

Mom puts a finger to her lips. "I don't want Zeyde to worry. They laid me off today. I told you things were slow at the restaurant."

"Yes, but—"

"I was the last hired, Ben. First to be let go. That's how it works sometimes."

"But . . ."

Mom sinks in her chair, like her bones are dissolving. "We just have to make it till I pass that test. In the meantime, I'll look for another job, but things are hard out there. No one seems to be hiring."

I think of Dad's galaxy on my bedroom ceiling. Of not going to sleep under it anymore. "Mom, we just need five hundred dollars before the end of the month. Right?"

"Right. But how am I going to do that with no job?"

I pat Mom's wild hair and channel my inner Dad. "We'll find a way."

Mom looks at me and smiles, but tears are slipping down her cheeks, like when it's raining but the sun's shining.

"It'll work out," I tell Mom, thinking of the candy money I plan to give her Friday—three hundred dollars. When she sees that, she'll know I'll be able to earn the other two hundred the following week, and we'll be okay until she can pass the test and start working at Mr. Daniels's accounting firm. It'll give us plenty of time before the November 2 deadline to pay what we owe. And, who knows, maybe I'll win the grand prize in the Royal-T contest for my slogan, and we won't have to worry about money again.

Zeyde comes back and sets the table for dinner.

I make the salad, and the three of us eat Mrs. Schneckle's noodle casserole and salad in dead silence.

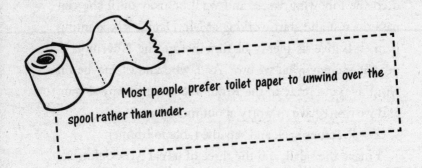

Most people prefer toilet paper to unwind over the spool rather than under.

Thursday, October 15, in the locker room, Angus Andrews buys three candy bars, but something doesn't feel right. I'm uncomfortable when he watches me put his three dollars into my backpack.

Something also doesn't smell right, but that's just Angus's BO.

I manage to sell out by the end of the school day and not get caught.

I'll be so glad when I hand the money to Mom tomorrow and see her face, when she realizes we'll make it after all. Three hundred this week. Two hundred next week, and we've got it made until Mom comes through by passing her test with flying colors.

I just have to get through tomorrow—Friday—and I'll be done selling for the week.

I can't believe this is actually going to work out!

. . .

Friday, October 16 . . .

Besides the hundred candy bars in my backpack, I've stashed all the money I made so far in a secret pocket in there as well. It felt great to take the money from my sock drawer and put it in my backpack. The stack of ones is too thick to keep in my pockets. By the end of the day today, if all goes according to plan, there will be three hundred dollars in the secret pocket in my backpack.

Three hundred beautiful, crumpled dollar bills to hand to Mom. I can't wait to see her face when I give it to her. My plan is to ask Toothpick to borrow his phone so I can text Mom and ask her to meet me at the Country Club Diner after school. I know when I give her all that money, she'll be okay with us using a little of it to have another celebration meal. We'll order all of Dad's favorite foods and talk about how awesome it is that we'll be able to pay Mr. Katz in time so we won't get kicked out.

Mom and I are a team—Team Epstein—and I know Dad would be proud.

I pat the place on my backpack where I've hidden the money. I want to kiss it for luck, like I do with my sweepstakes entries, but I'm in school and there's no way I'm doing that!

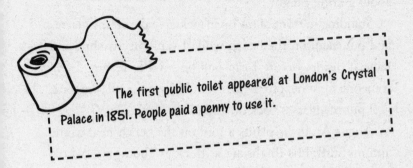

The first public toilet appeared at London's Crystal Palace in 1851. People paid a penny to use it.

By the time I arrive at the locker room, I feel terrific, because between my morning classes and lunchtime in the cafeteria, I've sold all but twelve candy bars.

The locker room is noisy as kids yell to each other across the rows and locker doors slam. It smells like BO, but that's probably because Angus Andrews is near me. I mean, it smells anyway, because it's a locker room, but Angus's odor eclipses everyone else's. He must bathe in garlic or something worse!

As I work the combination on my lock, I wish someone would buy all twelve candy bars right now so I could be done for today and forget about it for a while. It would be nice to go through the rest of the day without worrying about getting caught.

Standing in front of my open locker, I take off my glasses and put them on the bench while I yank off my shirt and hang it inside. Before I can pull on my PE T-shirt, I feel someone right next to me. Or should I say I smell someone.

I put my glasses back on and turn.

Angus Andrews plants a foot on the bench next to me and my stuff. His thighs are as thick as Toothpick's whole body. (Of course, that's not saying much.) Without meaning to, I take a step backward, away from Angus. Away from my stuff.

"So," Angus says. "Do you have any candy bars left for me?"

"Sure," I say. I hope he wants to buy all twelve. But I don't like him standing so close.

I notice fewer locker doors slamming. The large room feels too quiet.

Angus moves close enough to me that I notice the odor of onions on his breath. It smells like cologne compared to his overwhelming BO.

I force my stomach to settle from the noxious odors. Vomiting on Angus's sneakers would probably be bad form ... plus then he wouldn't want to buy the rest of my candy bars. A lone locker door slams, and I wonder if Toothpick is still in here. I barely keep from calling out his name.

Angus inches forward. "So?"

A bad feeling washes over me. Something tells me to get out, to run like my *tuchis* is on fire. I wonder if the warning feeling is somehow coming from Dad. I look up but see only dirty ceiling tiles and some wads of dried toilet paper stuck up there. I have to ignore the feeling so I can sell the rest of the candy bars and make it to the gym before Coach forces me to run humiliation laps again.

Besides, if I tried to run away now, Angus could catch me in a nanosecond by reaching out his massive, hairy arm. And I'd look like an idiot running off when nothing has happened, especially when I'm not wearing a shirt. Angus is just standing there. Too close, but just standing. That's what I tell myself to feel better about this sensation rushing over my spine, like an unexpected wave at the beach near Aunt Abby's condo. *Absolutely nothing has happened. Yet.*

Besides, there's no way I'm running off and leaving my backpack behind.

I glance at my backpack, which is closer to Angus than it is to me.

Sweat prickles in my armpits, and soon I'll probably smell as bad as Angus does. *He just wants to buy some candy bars,* I tell myself, but thinking that doesn't make the panicky feeling go away.

I take a baby step toward my backpack when I hear sneakers flapping against the floor and the door to the gym creak open. That's the last noise I hear in the locker room, other than my own heartbeat, which sounds as loud in my ears as Zeyde's seismic snoring.

"Um, I think we're going to be late, Angus." But I know he doesn't care. He's usually late for gym. "So, I'd better, um, get going." I almost add "Okay?" but don't want to appear like I'm asking his permission. Because I'm not. I just want to get to the gym. Safely. I don't even care if I have to run humiliation laps at this point.

Then I tell myself to knock it off, because nothing is actually wrong. It's all in my head. Or my gut, because that worried feeling's settled there.

Angus smiles. A scary smile. An I-should-be-in-a-horror-movie-because-I'm-about-to-annihilate-you-and-enjoy-it smile. I think Toothpick should cast Angus as the supervillain in one of his films. He'd be totally believable.

My legs feel weak and wobbly, like wet kugel noodles. "So," I say, pointing feebly to my locker. "I've got to get my stuff."

In one quick motion, Angus slams my locker door and snaps and spins my combination lock.

Something clicks in my heart. "Um, Angus, I need my, um, shirt." I hate the whiny way my voice sounds.

"You got any of those candy bars left?" Angus asks.

It'll be okay. It'll be okay. It'll— "Sure," I say, inching closer to my stuff lying on the bench. I pull a candy bar from my backpack.

"Thanks," Angus says, grabbing the candy bar and going back to his locker.

While I have a little breathing space, I send a mental message to Toothpick to find some reason to come back into the locker room. Two against one has got to be better than just me and Angus. Anything has got to be better than just me and Angus.

Toothpick must not receive my mental message, because he doesn't come back. I even try thinking to Coach that I'm still in here, but he must be too busy teaching his new Fun and Fit Workout (not fun) to notice. I don't hear a door open, a toilet flush, a locker slam closed. Nothing.

It's just me and Angus and my backpack, which is lying exposed on the bench. My backpack, which contains nearly three hundred dollars and eleven slightly melted candy bars.

When Angus forces something into my palm, my whole body tenses. But I allow my fingers to uncurl, and I see a crumpled dollar bill. That's when I let out a breath I hadn't realized I'd been holding. *Angus just wanted to buy a candy bar. He was messing with me when he slammed my locker door.*

"Well, I gotta get ready for gym now," I say, inching toward my locker.

Angus heads me off and blocks my locker. "Actually, I'm reeeeaaaal hungry, Ben. You have any more?"

"Sure," I say, the weak feeling in my legs creeping up through the rest of my body. "I definitely have more."

I pull out the rest of the candy bars and lay them on the bench. I almost say *You can have them for free, just leave me alone,* but my need for money overrides my need to stay alive and I say, "Eleven more bucks."

Part of me still thinks this will turn out okay. Maybe

Angus has enough cash to buy the rest of my candy bars, and I can be done for the day and get to gym.

Angus throws the candy bars into his locker.

I hold out my hand, trying to keep it steady. "Eleven bucks."

When Angus stands there, I say a little louder, "Eleven bucks . . . please."

"Eleven bucks, please, huh?" Angus steps toward me.

"Yeah," I squeak, and wonder if I should say "please" again.

Another step. Too close.

I hold my ground, but I'm sweating in places I didn't know I could sweat, which Angus can probably tell, because I'm not wearing a shirt.

"Yeah," Angus says, "I seen you putting the money in there yesterday. I'll bet there's a ton of money in that backpack. You probably don't really need my eleven bucks. Do you?"

A weird noise gurgles up from my throat.

"How much money do you have in there, wuss?" Angus's eyes get really wide. "A lot. Right?"

A whiff of onions and BO hits me along with his words, and my stomach flops.

That's when I know.

I'm screwed out of the last of my candy bars from today. He's not going to pay me the eleven bucks, and I paid fifty cents for each of them at WaWa. *This is so unfair!* Angus probably doesn't even need the money like I do. I consider slipping past him and grabbing my candy bars back from his locker, but I know I'm not going to do that.

I'm too much of a wuss to do that. Angus is right.

"I mean," he says, "it's not like you can tell Sheffield about this, because technically"—he gets even closer, and I feel his damp, stinkin' breath on my face—"you're not supposed to be selling them. Are you? You can't say one word about this to Sheffield." Angus looks around. "Or anyone else. Right?"

My stomach has the same feeling I remember having the moment I plunged over the crest of the giant roller coaster at Great Adventure—when I won tickets from radio station WMMR. Except I'm standing perfectly still now. The only thing moving on me is sweat, which is running in rivulets down my sides from every pore in my armpits.

I wish the bell would ring, signaling the end of gym, and everyone would flood back into the locker room, but I know the period isn't even halfway over. Not even a quarter over, probably, even though it feels like I've been in this lousy locker room with Angus for a month. And not a short month like February either. A long, dark, dreary month, like January or March.

"But you said . . ." The weakness in my trembling voice matches the weakness in my body, and it embarrasses me.

Angus laughs, and I realize I was an idiot for thinking he would ever buy the rest of my candy bars. Now I'm out twelve bars with only one sweaty dollar in my palm to show for it. I know eleven bucks isn't a ton of money, but it's not right for Angus to steal my stuff. Anger fills me, and I clench my fists.

Angus moves even closer. He smells so bad, I'm afraid I'll barf.

I want to shove him away, to grab my backpack and run, like I should have done when I first got that warning feeling. I want to pound Angus in the face for taking my candy bars and ripping me off. I want—

"Wuss," Angus whispers, standing directly in front of me.

The tip of my nose almost touches his chin. I can see blackheads in the pores on his face. "Sure, sure," I say, survival instinct kicking in. "You can have them, Angus. It's cool."

A dose of stupidity surges through me, and I lunge for my backpack, hoping I'm fast enough that Angus won't realize what I'm doing.

He realizes.

With strong, fat fingers, Angus grabs my wrist with his right hand and my backpack with his left. "Yeah, right!" Angus says, and throws my backpack—*my* backpack with *my* money inside!—into *his* locker. And slams the door.

Then he twirls the lock dial.

Game over.

My money in the secret pocket in my backpack is trapped inside Angus's smelly locker.

I manage a feeble "Hey!" before Angus's thick palm lands on the middle of my bare chest, and he shoves me backward.

The back of my head connects with someone's lock so

hard I actually see stars—little pulses of light. Not the good kind either, like from my ceiling. The I-might-pass-out-on-the-locker-room-floor kind.

I take a breath—of sweat and locker room stink—and a small step forward, rubbing my sore head, holding back tears that threaten to erupt like Mount Vesuvius.

While I'm dazed from the clonk to the back of my head, Angus snatches the sweaty dollar bill from my hand, scratching me in the process. *As if the humiliation and head injury aren't enough, now I'll probably get rabies.*

"That's mine," Angus says, jabbing me in the chest with his fat finger. He presses so hard, it feels like his finger might break through my breastbone and plunge directly into my heart.

A weird noise bubbles from my throat that I hope sounds like the words "All right" but probably sounds more like an animal that's been wounded in the wild and emits its final feeble cry.

The inside of my head swirls, and I feel like I'm going to *plotz*. That's when a brilliant idea pops into my addled brain. "Angus," I say. "I have medicine in that backpack. If I don't get it, I might, like, die."

"Yeah, right." He looks at me and tilts his head. "What do you think I am? A moron?"

Yes! I can tell Angus is wondering, though. . . .

I have to get my money back!

"No, really," I say, pushing my glasses up on my nose and hoping I sound as honest as George Washington. "I need that medicine." I make my hand shake so it looks like I'm already getting sick.

Angus squints at me. "Well, let's just see," he says, turning the dial on his lock.

When he opens his locker, I feel so much relief I'm afraid I'm going to wet myself. It takes all my energy not to grab my backpack and run.

Angus starts unzipping pockets on my backpack, and he pulls out a couple loose Tic Tacs that were in one of the pockets. "This?" he asks.

They were from Toothpick from a long time ago. I'm so glad they were in there. I nod, hoping he'll believe the Tic Tacs are actually medicine. *He is a moron!*

"Here." He tosses them, and I scramble on the floor for them so he thinks they're really important. After I swallow the Tic Tacs, I don't know what I'm going to do next, but at least I'll have fresh, minty breath when I do it.

"Ooooh," Angus says. "What's this?"

He reaches into the pocket inside another pocket—my secret hiding place—and pulls out the fat stack of crumpled cash.

And I know I'm in even worse shape than before I tried the stupid medicine trick. I should tackle him and try to get my money back, but I don't. Because I'm a coward.

"Thanks, wuss! I can totally use this." He tosses the nearly three hundred dollars into his locker and spins the dial on his lock. My backpack lies empty and useless on the bench.

In an explosion of foul onion breath, Angus spits: "Don't.

Tell. Anyone." For emphasis, he pokes me hard in the chest with each word.

I shake my throbbing head left to right. *Don't cry. Don't cry.* "I won't," I say, answering Angus and the voice in my head at the same time.

Angus sizes me up. "Or else . . ."

I'm still shaking my head side to side.

Apparently satisfied, Angus nods once and takes off.

I don't move. I don't even breathe, in case he comes back. If he hasn't finished with me yet. Part of me can't believe it's finally over.

I collapse onto the bench and touch my backpack. My stupid, empty backpack.

The only thing I have to show for all my hard work is a throbbing headache in the back of my head, a scratch on my hand that looks like it's raging with rabies infection and zero cash.

I worked so hard for that money!

I picture Mom going to court and having to explain that she doesn't have enough to keep us from getting evicted. That she doesn't have the lousy five hundred dollars we need because of what Angus did.

Sitting in the foul-smelling locker room on the bench next to my empty backpack, I know with absolute certainty that I'm done selling candy bars. I can't deal with this. I can't work this hard only to have Angus take my money.

Store closed. Out of business.

The end.

In 2004 in Omaha, Nebraska, a man escaped prison by waving a fake gun made from toilet paper, tape and black ink. Four days later, he was captured and taken back to prison.

I check around the rows of lockers and, seeing no one, grip Angus Andrews's lock and pull it with all my might again and again. It doesn't open. I try different combinations, listening to the tumblers inside, but the lock holds firm. I yank on it really hard a few more times, but that only hurts my sore hand. No matter how desperately I try, the lock doesn't give.

Locks are stubborn like that.

So I kick the bottom locker and scream a word I'm not supposed to.

From outside the locker room, a deep voice bellows, "Anyone in there?" Coach's voice. *Why did I kick that stupid locker and scream?* My heart goes into overdrive, but I press my lips together and wait silently. *A little late, aren't you, Coach?*

Sitting on the bench again, hoping Coach doesn't come in, I put my head in the crook of my elbow. The back of my head throbs like an aching drum. My hand hurts from where Angus scratched me. Even my toes feel fractured from kicking the stupid locker.

I hate you, Angus Andrews! I hate your stupid, stinkin', miserable guts!

I glare at his locker door like I have superpowers that will make it fly open so I can get my money and give it to Mom, like I planned. Our plan. The Grand Plan.

Mom. I've let her down big-time, and she doesn't even know it.

I open my own locker and put my regular shirt back on, being careful of my glasses and of the place Angus repeatedly jammed his fat finger into my chest. It's already blossoming into a bruise.

I grab my stupid empty backpack and go inside a bathroom stall.

There's graffiti on the interior stall walls and door, and I decide I'll stay there reading the dumb graffiti until gym is over, because there's no way I'm going out to the gym now to run humiliation laps. No way! I realize I can't stay in the stall, though, because the last thing I want is to be here when Angus returns. He might not be done slamming my head into lockers.

"Jerk!"

There's some wet stuff on my cheeks, so I pull off toilet paper to wipe it away. One thin square rips off. I try again and get another single, useless square. And another. I throw the pieces in the toilet and wipe my cheeks with the back of my hand. "Why can't I get decent toilet paper anywhere?"

I shoulder my backpack and walk out of the locker room toward the gym.

Some kids are doing push-ups, then jumping up in between and doing more push-ups. Other kids jog in place, then do jumping jacks. *Looks like fun.*

I hide behind the wall near the doorway, put both arms through my backpack straps and peek out again.

Coach is at the far end of the gym, showing some guy how to do a proper push-up. I glance at the door to the right that leads into school and the door to my immediate left that leads outside to the track and fields behind school.

Outside.

Not realizing I've made a choice, I start moving.

Left.

I'm at the door, slamming into the bar with my hip and praying it's not alarmed or locked. I'm surprised when the heavy metal door flies open and cool air rushes in. But the door makes a lot of noise when it opens. I'm sure everyone is looking at me now. I feel their stares on my back. Even Angus is probably staring, but I don't turn around.

And I don't look back when Coach blows his whistle, then bellows, "You. By the door. Stop!"

I don't stop.

"I said *stop*!"
I don't.
I

       R

             U

                  N!

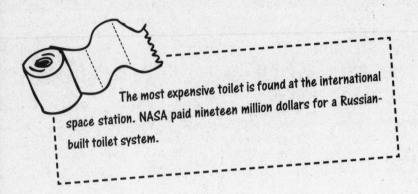

The most expensive toilet is found at the international space station. NASA paid nineteen million dollars for a Russian-built toilet system.

I pound across the field to the track. Cool air whooshing past, I run along one side of the track faster than I ever have in PE, even when Coach was timing us and it counted for a grade. Gravel sprays up behind my sneakers.

Coach must be chasing me now. I brace myself for the blast of his whistle or his body slamming into mine and knocking me to the ground, although the only footsteps I hear are my own. The only breathing I hear is mine.

Still, I don't slow until I crash into the fence that surrounds our school. Across from the fence are row houses, but nobody is outside. *Thank goodness!*

I do something I didn't know I could: I climb the fence,

even though the metal bites into my fingers. Then I drop to the other side—off school grounds—and I keep running.

Past row houses and intersections and stores. Past old ladies with shopping bags and people walking dogs. Past a SEPTA bus, stopped at the corner, and the playground with the purple-dinosaur slide, where I used to go with Bubbe Mary and Zeyde Jake when I was little.

I run. And run. And keep running farther and farther away . . . from that jerk, Angus, and all he took from me.

I run until the bones in my legs feel like they might splinter and my lungs shred.

When I finally slow and bend forward to catch my breath, a cold wind whips across my back, turning my sweat icy. I wish I'd stopped at my regular locker to get my jacket, but I don't even have that. I stand tall and wrap my arms around myself.

I hate you, Angus Andrews!

Even though it's not really *that* cold outside—it's only October—my teeth clack together a few times. And I realize it's because I'm fist-squeezing, lips-pressing angry. Angus Andrews ruined everything for us.

Because of him we're going to get kicked out. With Zeyde!

Then the anger—mean and fast—slices around my brain like a red-hot blade and finds another target.

The real target.

I feel instantly guilty, and my heart aches so hard I

double over. But I can't stop the wave of feelings. I'm incredibly pissed. And the person I'm pissed at is my dad, even though he didn't do anything wrong. Except die.

The logical part of my brain knows it wasn't Dad's fault. He would have stuck around if he could have, but my racing heart knows it's all his fault. Since Dad died, everything's changed. For the worse. Even our lousy freakin' toilet paper.

I'm so angry I could rocket my fist through a brick wall. Or Angus's head, which is kind of the same thing. I bend all the way over, pull my elbow back and punch the sidewalk. I manage to scrape the knuckles on my right hand hard enough to remind me of all the other places on my body that hurt.

The back of my head still pulses where Angus slammed it into the lock. My hand throbs where Angus scratched me and probably gave me rabies. And every millimeter of my skin is clammy, even though on the inside I'm boiling and roiling with rage.

All those angry feelings shift and morph into something else. Something that floats up from my belly and catches in my throat. Something that makes my body feel so heavy I can hardly stand anymore. My legs are cement. My head's a boulder.

I drop to the bottom step in front of someone's house, put my stupid boulder head in my hands and sniff hard, because I know one thing: I, Benjamin Epstein, am an epic failure.

I failed to defend myself against Angus.

I failed to get that money to Mom, which means I failed to keep us from getting kicked out.

I failed Zeyde, because when we get kicked out, he won't have a place to live or he'll have to go back to Aunt Abby's place and her fourteen smelly cats.

Worst of all, I failed the one person I couldn't afford to fail.

"You were counting on me, Dad. I let you down."

Looking at the cloudy autumn sky, I let out a slow, defeated breath.

Even though I know the stars are up there and I just can't see them because it's daytime, it feels like they don't exist anymore. It feels like there's not a single star left in the universe. Not a single glow-in-the-dark star left on my bedroom ceiling at home.

Not a star left anywhere, because I just extinguished the last one.

I blink and whisper to the stupid, starless sky, "I'm sorry, Dad."

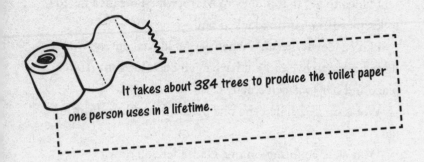

It takes about 384 trees to produce the toilet paper one person uses in a lifetime.

I force myself to get off the steps, because I don't want someone to come out of the house behind me and ask if I'm okay—*Because I'm not!*—or tell me to get off their property and go back to school.

Since I couldn't deal with any of that right now, I keep moving.

I don't even know where I'm going, just that I'm walking as far away from Angus as I can. Unfortunately, I'm also walking away from my money. He'll probably have it spent by day's end on some stupid video games or something.

And since I can't tell Mr. Sheffield what I was doing, because I wasn't supposed to be doing it, there's no way I can get my money back. There's no one I can tell. Nothing I can do.

I kick the back tire of a parked car, but it just hurts my foot.

I wish I could walk away from myself and my problems. Just keep walking and never go home. But then what would Mom do?

Mom.

I can't tell Mom what happened either. She'll be crazy mad at Angus for hurting me and stealing our money. Our rent money. She'll probably go to school and tell Mr. Sheffield, and that would be even worse. If Angus got in trouble with Mr. Sheffield, he'd make me pay for that every single day for the rest of the year. And it's a long way to June.

I decide I won't even tell Toothpick. It's too embarrassing how I let Angus hurt me and take my money.

I keep walking.

There are fewer houses. Bigger houses. More trees.

I keep going, along sidewalks, up and down hills.

When I realize where I am, it feels like a complete surprise, but part of me must have meant to come here all along.

My leg muscles cramp from traveling so far. I massage them briefly and continue past the ornate iron gates. I walk beyond the wide entrance and begin the trek along the winding driveway, bordered by grass and tall pines. And rows and rows of gray . . .

Shalom Memorial Park Cemetery.

I think about the people under all those headstones. So many headstones. Different sizes, different words and dates on them. I think about the sad kids and moms and aunts and *zeydes* and . . .

Heartache washes over me like a wave—a tsunami—but I keep trudging forward.

Up the hill and around a curve in the road, past where Bubbe Mary is buried.

My heart knows the way.

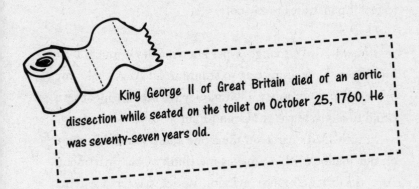

King George II of Great Britain died of an aortic dissection while seated on the toilet on October 25, 1760. He was seventy-seven years old.

Mom and I have visited Dad's grave plenty of times, but I've never come alone.

It feels like a punch to the gut to see the cold, gray stone with his name engraved—TODD EPSTEIN—and the dates of his birth and death. Mom also had them write LOVING HUSBAND AND FATHER. YOU'RE UP AMONG THE STARS NOW, which is kind of perfect. I know Zeyde paid for the headstone and the funeral, because I overheard Mom talking to Aunt Abby about it.

There are a few small rocks on top of the headstone, which means Mom's been here.

I touch the stone but don't feel anything except cold, dry rock. I don't know what I expected to feel. I wish I could feel Dad's hand on my shoulder one more time. The ache to feel it penetrates to my core.

Dad.

I breathe in heaving gasps, knowing how much I let him down. Knowing I was so stupid to let Angus take my money. Our rent money. That money would have meant we could finally achieve our Grand Plan.

I touch Dad's name on the stone and think of his name on our mailbox, which makes me think of our apartment. And the bright orange eviction notice plastered on the door. *We can't get kicked out!* I have to come up with something else. Something that will save us.

But I'm so tired. There's nothing left in me. No more ideas. No more plans. No more . . . hope. Every glimmer of it was extinguished when Angus smashed my head into the lock and stole our money.

I sink down and lean my back against the edge of Dad's stone, like he's holding me up somehow.

And while I sit there—numb and hollow—some awful thing pushes open a door in my brain. A door I don't want opened—a door I never wanted opened again—but I haven't the energy to hold it closed any longer.

A memory seeps from its hiding place, corrosive and painful.

It happened in our living room/dining room/kitchen.

Two deliverymen managed to squeeze a full-size hospital bed into that space—the kind of bed with gray side rails and wheels underneath.

The bed arrived just before Dad returned from his last stay at the hospital—fifth floor, cancer patients. Many patients were bald and curled small in their beds, like Dad.

Mom and I spent a lot of time in Dad's hospital room. I was in sixth grade then. I did homework there, and sometimes a nurse would give me a plastic cup of vanilla ice cream with a flat wooden spoon. Once in a while, the three of us watched TV together. But that usually turned into Mom and me watching, because Dad slept a lot. Mom was supposed to be working, but she stayed with Dad.

All Dad talked about when he was in the hospital— when he talked at all—was wanting to come home. I remember him grabbing Mom's wrist once and pleading, "Shelley, please. Get me out of here."

When Dad was finally back at our apartment in the hospital bed in the living room/dining room/kitchen, he slept most of the time.

Mom stayed beside him, holding his hand, sleeping on the couch near him, and once I saw her in the bed with Dad, curled up next to him. Her eyelids were open, but his were closed. She stared so intently at his face, it looked like she was memorizing him.

One time Mom left me with Dad for a few minutes so she could shower.

While sitting beside him, I kept thinking about how different Dad looked from the photo of him on the beach that Mom had near her bed. He looked nothing like that strong guy showing off his muscles. In the hospital bed in our living room/dining room/kitchen, Dad was whisper thin. His face looked like a skull with skin stretched over it. And his voice had evaporated to a raspy whisper, too. I needed to lean close to hear when he talked.

Even though Dad was thin—except for his belly, which protruded like it was stuffed with a basketball—I didn't realize how bad things were.

I still went to school and to Toothpick's house and everything, but Mom must have known, because she spent every minute with Dad. She stopped going to work at the accounting firm, where she'd worked as an accountant's assistant for just over a year. She'd already used up the time she was allowed to take off, but still, she stayed with Dad. Even when her boss, nasty Ms. Jenkins, told her she'd lose her job if she didn't return to work, Mom stayed with Dad. Even when Mrs. Schneckle said she'd take over and keep Dad company so Mom could at least go to the grocery store, Mom stayed beside Dad. When Zeyde begged her to get out, to take a break for a little while, Mom didn't budge.

Mom even made sure I was next to Dad when she took a shower. She didn't want him to be alone even for a minute. So I was next to Dad while Mom showered this one day.

Dad strained to talk to me, grimacing with effort.

I remember wishing I could help him, wishing Mom were there to translate, in case I missed any of his words. All I could do was lean close, hold my breath and pay attention.

Dad smelled sweet, like the powder Mom sometimes used.

"I love you, Ben," his whisper-words said.

Chills rippled through my body, like it somehow knew what my mind couldn't possibly understand: that would be the last time I'd hear Dad say those words.

"I love you, too," I said, desperate for him to know how much I meant it.

Dad let out a ragged breath. "I'm counting on you."

I nodded once, still close to his whisper-breath mouth.

"I'm counting . . ." Dad coughed and squeezed his eyelids against the pain, then opened them and looked at me. "You need to . . . take care of . . ." He grabbed my arm, except his hand was so weak I hardly felt the pressure of it, which made me sad, because I wasn't supposed to be way stronger than my dad at eleven years old.

". . . your mom."

Dad looked at me with eyes that were clear for the first time in a long time, so I focused one hundred percent on what he was saying.

"Take care of . . . your mom. I'm counting on you . . . Ben."

"I will," I tell him. "I promise. I will." I didn't even know what that would mean, but I'd say yes to anything. I'd do anything. If only . . .

Dad's hand slipped from my arm, his eyelids closed and his whispered words swirled around my brain in an endless loop: *I'm counting on you, Ben. I'm counting on you, Ben. I'm counting on you, Ben.*

Mom came out of the bathroom, toweling off her hair. "Everything okay?"

Dad was so sick he could barely talk, and he slept most of the time. How could *anything* be okay? I nodded, hoping Mom couldn't see tears sliding down my stupid cheeks.

I swivel around now, touch Dad's headstone and cross my arms tightly over my chest. The back of my head still aches from Angus shoving me into the lock. But what's going on inside my head is much more painful. Dad's words continue to swirl around my mind, like they never stopped: *I'm counting on you, Ben. I'm counting on you, Ben. I'm counting on you, Ben.*

I didn't know it then, but those were the last words Dad would ever say to me.

He stopped breathing the next night. Mom was with him, of course. I was sleeping in my room under his painted galaxy.

I didn't go to school that day or the next. I didn't return until after we were done sitting shivah for him.

Even though Dad's gone, I've carried his words with me ever since, in a heavy bag attached to my heart.

The problem is, I *haven't* taken care of my mom. I've let everything fall apart. I didn't follow through with Dad's Grand Plan. I was supposed to help get Mom through her last test so she could pass and get that job at Mr. Daniels's firm as an actual accountant. Accountants make a lot more money than accountant's assistants, like the position she held at the other accounting firm. Everything would have been fine if we could have just made it until then. But now we're going to get kicked out, because I let Angus take the money we needed to pay Mr. Katz.

I failed my dad with his very last request of me.

What kind of person does that? I wish he'd never asked that of me. But he did. And I failed.

I stand and search the ground for a couple small stones to place on top of Dad's headstone. After I drop them near the ones Mom must have put there, I whisper, "I'm sorry, Dad." I put my cheek on top of the cool stone. "I'm sorry I let you down."

Then I begin the long walk home.

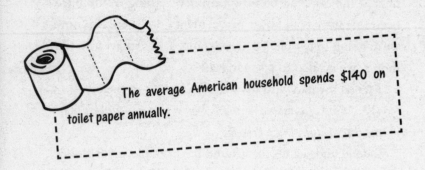

The average American household spends $140 on toilet paper annually.

Inside our apartment building, I don't even stop at the mailbox. I don't have the energy, and I don't care what's inside anymore.

Walking up the seven steps from the foyer to our apartment feels like climbing Mount Kilimanjaro. Somehow I arrive at our front door, to the awful orange notice where Mrs. Schneckle wrote *Mr. Katz is a shmendrik,* and I let myself in. Every time I see the notice, it's like a punch in the gut. I wish it would go away.

All I want is to go into my room, curl up under my comforter and watch Barkley swim around his tank. He won't judge me for being a failure. He won't remind me that I didn't keep my final promise to Dad. He'll just swim and eat and poop and keep me good company, like Dad said he would.

Even if he isn't a dog.

Inside the living room/dining room/kitchen, I drop my stupid empty backpack on the couch and walk down the hallway to my room.

I'm glad the apartment is quiet. I need to be alone right now.

I collapse onto my bed and am about to kick off my sneakers when I see it—the roll of lousy, gray toilet paper.

"No! No!"

I drop down on one knee in front of my desk and grip the sides of the tank. "Barkley!"

The tank's lid is open, and the lousy, gray toilet paper is inside, lying on the blue layer of gravel, leaning against the castle. The toilet paper has sucked up almost all the water in the tank, except for a few inches at the bottom.

"Zeyde!" He was probably trying to make the toilet paper softer and didn't realize Barkley was in there. "Barkley."

I pull out the bloated, dripping roll and throw it on Zeyde's bed, not caring if I ruin anything.

Barkley's swimming slowly through toilet paper bits, which look like minnows. I want to scoop the tiny pieces of paper out, because they're clouding Barkley's water, but I don't know how to do it. There's so many of them.

I want to scoop Barkley out and put him in fresh, clean water so he can breathe, but I can't do that either. He needs conditioned or distilled water, and there's no time for that right now. The shock of being dropped into plain tap water might kill him.

And I can't do that.

I look up briefly at the galaxy, wishing for the millionth time my dad were here to help me, to tell me what to do.

As I look more closely inside the tank, I realize Barkley's not swimming anymore.

He's floating.

Maybe he never was swimming.

His black eyes stare at me as if to say, *Do something. I'm counting on you, Ben.*

"Barkley?" I croak.

I tap the outside of his tank, even though you're not supposed to do that.

Then I grab his package of fish food and carefully sprinkle three pellets on top of the water. Only three. It's bad to overfeed a fish, so I'm always careful to give him only two or three pellets twice each day.

Barkley usually darts to the food the moment I sprinkle it in.

Now the pellets lay on top of the polluted water, floating among the toilet paper bits.

Barkley doesn't dart after it.

He doesn't move at all.

That's when I know.

I look at the stupid stars on my stupid ceiling, then back

down into the tank, where Barkley floats among the toilet paper bits.

"Oh, Barkley . . ."

"Who's Barkley?"

I jerk around.

Zeyde's standing in the bedroom doorway. He looks so happy. He walks over to the daybed, picks up the bloated, wet toilet paper roll and laughs.

"It's not funny!" I scream. "You killed my fish!"

Zeyde's eyes go wide. "I . . . I . . . I'm just coming back from Mrs. Schneckle's. She made cinnamon cookies and coffee." He kisses his fingertips. "Delicious, *boychik*!"

"I don't care what she made! Did you hear me? You killed my fish! You murdered Barkley!"

Zeyde tilts his head. "Who's Barkley?"

A wave of heat courses through my head, and I feel like I'm going to *plotz*.

I look at Barkley, floating in the toilet paper bits. I look at Zeyde, his mouth open. "How could you do that?" I shout.

The door to our apartment opens and Mom calls, "Benjamin?"

"What?" I bark.

Mom strides down the hall and stands in the doorway of my room with a hand on her hip. "I got a call from school today."

I inhale sharply. "Zeyde killed my fish."

"I . . . I . . . ," Zeyde stammers.

Mom marches in, looks at the tank, then at Zeyde, who's still holding the toilet paper. "Oh, Dad." Mom puts a hand over her mouth, then drops it. "Please tell me you didn't."

"I was just making it softer," he whispers.

Mom grips my shoulders. "Look at me, Ben."

I don't.

"Benjamin Epstein, look at me."

My head is throbbing, and I don't think it's from Angus having slammed it into the lock. I have trouble focusing on Mom, even though she's standing right in front of me.

"I'm going to take care of this," Mom says.

"You can't," I say, not sure if I'm talking about Barkley or Angus stealing our rent money. My head feels like it's stuffed with toilet paper. "It's too late."

I look over at Zeyde and scream, "How could you kill my fish?" *Barkley was from Dad!*

Mom tightens her grip on my shoulders and looks into my eyes. "Ben, you need to get some air. Go take a walk or something."

A few tears dribble out. "I don't want to walk." I don't tell Mom I just walked about a million miles and am about to fall over.

She pulls me to her for a hug that practically suffocates me.

It makes me think of Barkley, suffocating from all that lousy toilet paper floating in his tank. It makes me think of Dad, near the end, when each breath sounded like a struggle.

I sob once and my whole body shudders.

Mom pulls me even tighter. "In fact," she whispers into my hair, "I want you to go to Michael's house. I'll call his dad to make sure it's okay."

I nod, snot dripping from my nose.

"Stay there tonight," Mom says. "I didn't realize it, but . . ." She pulls back from me and looks at the fish tank. "You need a break, Ben. You need a break from everything. Don't you?"

I nod and wipe my nose on my sleeve.

"We'll talk about what happened at school later."

Those words make my stomach cramp.

"I can walk you there," Zeyde says, like he's trying to make up for what he did.

Mom and I both turn to look at him.

"I'm fine," I say, even though I'm hot and achy. "I can go by myself," I practically snarl at Zeyde.

Mom tousles my hair. "Go, Benjamin. Go now."

I turn and walk out, without saying so long to Mom or Zeyde. Without saying good-bye to Barkley.

According to some studies, more than 70 percent of the world's population doesn't use toilet paper because of tradition, religion or expense.

Shivering in the night air, I find myself standing in front of a familiar door and have the energy to knock only once.

But it's enough.

The door opens, like it has a hundred times before.

"Your mom called," Mr. Taylor says. "Come in." He enfolds me in his massive arms for a hug. His bearded chin rests on top of my head. "Oh, Ben. I'm so sorry."

I allow myself to fall limp in Mr. Taylor's embrace.

He half walks me, half carries me to the couch in their living room. "You don't look so great, pal. Here. Lie down." He tucks a square pillow under my head. And I realize the back of my head doesn't hurt anymore. Nothing seems to hurt anymore. But I'm freezing.

Toothpick's eyes are wide as he watches his dad take care of me. There's a giant gash on his neck, and it takes me a second to realize it isn't real. I try to smile, but can't.

I try to say hi, but nothing comes out of my dust-dry mouth.

Toothpick bites his bottom lip. I think he looks like my mom when he does that. Maybe it is my mom and I'm hallucinating. Maybe . . .

I want to tell Toothpick I'm okay so he'll stop looking at me like that—like I'm dying or something—but I don't think I am okay. As I'm lying on the Taylors' couch, little stars of light explode behind my eyelids, but my eyelids are open.

I try to tell Toothpick and his dad I don't feel so good, that I'm dizzy and the room is spinning, but words don't come.

And everything goes dark.

• • •

Someone presses a glass to my lips. I sit and sip, vaguely aware that water's dripping down my chin and into my shirt, then I'm gulping like I'm in the desert and haven't had a drink for days.

Unfortunately, the water sloshing in my stomach makes me think of Barkley floating in the toilet paper water. And I vomit. All over myself. All over the Taylors' nice couch.

"It's okay," a deep voice says. "You just drank too fast, Ben."

I think it's Mr. Taylor's voice. But those tiny stars flash again, and it's hard to hang on to words or anything else.

• • •

Someone's saying my name really loudly and slapping a cold cloth across my forehead.

I blink, look through my glasses and see Toothpick standing over me.

He's out of focus, like I'm seeing him through a camera lens that isn't adjusted yet. Or through murky water. When Pick becomes clearer, there's a pretty bad injury on his neck. I wonder if we were in some kind of accident and we're in the hospital together.

My throat's sore, but I manage to say, "You don't look so good, Pick."

His hand goes to his neck and he smiles. "Look who's talking. You're the patient here."

"Am I in the hospital?"

"Heck, no. You're on our couch." Toothpick looks at me like I'm weird. "Are you okay, man? You're sort of scaring me."

I find the energy to nod.

"He's going to be fine," Mr. Taylor says, pressing the back of his thick hand against my forehead. "You have a fever, buddy," he tells me. "Your mom said it's okay to give you something for it. I'm sure you'll feel better in no time. You young guys get over these things fast."

I relax onto their couch, except the couch is kind of damp and so am I.

"Thank goodness I wasn't working tonight," he says.

I interrupt Mr. Taylor by burping, and they look panicked at first, then laugh.

"Thought you were going to barf again," Pick says.

His dad shoves Toothpick's shoulder. "Michael!"

"What?" Toothpick asks, rubbing his shoulder. "He's like a barfing machine."

That's why I'm damp. I must have puked. I hope I didn't ruin their couch. "Sorry."

"Not to worry," Mr. Taylor says, giving Toothpick the evil eye. "Ben, I'm going to call your mom again and tell her how you're doing. Then I'll get you some ginger ale and . . ."

"Mom."

"She told me what happened to your fish," Mr. Taylor says. "I'm sorry, son." And his strong hand is rubbing my shoulder, just like Dad used to do.

This makes me cry, but I wipe my cheeks and hope Toothpick doesn't notice.

Mr. Taylor wraps me in a thick blanket, and Toothpick sits next to me, away from the wet part of the couch, occasionally bumping his shoulder into mine and touching his fake wound.

And that's all. No questions. No talking.

I like it that way.

Mr. Taylor brings me a mug filled with ginger ale.

They watch me drink, which is kind of uncomfortable, but the bubbly soda feels good going down my dry, acidy throat.

Toothpick still has a worried expression on his face, and I realize I might look like one of the living dead from his movie-makeup magazines. Getting robbed in the locker room, walking about a million miles and losing one's pet all on the same lousy day can do that to a person.

Mr. Taylor pulls up a chair and sits in front of me while I sip the ginger ale.

"I called your mom."

I nod.

"She said to tell you she loves you and hopes you feel better soon." Mr. Taylor pats my knee. "I'm sure you'll be fine in no time."

I'm not so sure, but I'm glad Mom suggested I come here, even if Mr. Taylor and Toothpick are seeing what a mess my life is. What a mess I am.

"And she said you can sleep over, Ben. I mean, if you'd like to."

I want to tell Mr. Taylor I'd like that a lot, because I don't want to go home and see my dead fish again. But my throat is so tight I just nod and hope he understands how much I appreciate his offer. For once, I need someone to take care of *me*.

"Good." Mr. Taylor stands, then sits again. "Ben, if you're feeling up to it, after you get a good night's sleep, we'll be celebrating Michael's birthday tomorrow—Saturday."

I'd completely forgotten my best friend's birthday. I look at Toothpick and try to tell him I'm sorry with my eyes. "The usual?" I ask.

"Oh, yeah," Toothpick says, punching his skinny fist in the air. "The Mütter Museum."

Toothpick loves going to the Mütter Museum, and I do, too, but I didn't make it last year for his birthday, because Dad was so sick then.

"We'd love for you to join us, Ben." Mr. Taylor scratches his beard. "If you're feeling better. Or I could take you home in the morning, if you'd rather, but your mom said she wouldn't be there."

I wonder where Mom will be, now that she's not working. I guess she'll be looking for another lousy waitressing job, where she'll have to serve greasy bacon and coffee to ungrateful people who leave lousy tips swimming in puddles of syrup.

"What do you say?" Mr. Taylor's eyes look hopeful.

"Yeah," Toothpick says, bumping his shoulder into mine. "You have to go with us tomorrow, Ben. It wouldn't be the same without you. I really missed you last year."

I'm not sure I'll be up for the Mütter Museum tomorrow. I still feel warm and achy. And sad. But I don't want to disappoint Mr. Taylor since he's being so nice to me. And it's the least I can do for Toothpick, since I didn't even remember his birthday was tomorrow. "Sure," I say. "I'll go."

But as soon as the words leave my mouth, they feel like a mistake.

My throat hurts.

Toothpick smiles.

My eyes hurt.

He gives me a fist bump. "We'll have an awesome time."

My heart hurts.

Mr. Taylor reaches over and grabs me into a huge hug with my mug between us, and Toothpick pounds me on the back, which hurts and feels good at the same time.

After I'm done drinking my ginger ale—I take my time, because I don't want to throw up again—Mr. Taylor brings me a pair of Toothpick's pajamas to wear.

They're way too long, but I cuff the pant legs and sleeves.

Toothpick's dad actually tucks me into bed in their guest room, like I'm a little kid. It makes me feel safe. "I'll have your clothes washed and ready for you by tomorrow morning."

"Thanks, Mr. Taylor." *For everything.*

After he closes the door, I look up, almost expecting to see the stars on my ceiling; then I remember I'm not at home in our apartment. After the court date on November 2, we'll be out of our apartment for good. I can't imagine where we'll live, but I know it won't have stars on the ceiling, so I'd better get used to it.

I can always pry the plastic stars off my ceiling and bring them with us to our new place—wherever that will be. At least I'd have them, but I wouldn't have the important part of the galaxy: the comets, planets and moon—the part Dad painted.

It's strange, but the guest room in Toothpick's house is so quiet, I wish I could hear Zeyde's familiar rumbling snores. I think the sound would actually help me fall asleep tonight. But thinking of Zeyde reminds me of what happened to Barkley, and my stomach clenches like a fist. And that makes me think of what Angus did to me, what he took from me. From us.

Breathe, Benjamin. Stop thinking. Just breathe.

At least Zeyde's seismic snores would drown out the thoughts swirling through my mind, the ones making my heart pound with worry.

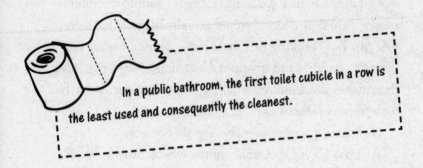

In a public bathroom, the first toilet cubicle in a row is the least used and consequently the cleanest.

When I wake, Mr. Taylor's standing over me, slurping from his coffee mug. "How you doing, champ?"

My eyelids feel swollen. My legs ache. My heart hurts. "Good," I lie, because what's the point of telling the truth? It won't change anything.

"Excellent," Mr. Taylor says, entirely too cheerful. "Your clothes are in the hallway bathroom, and breakfast is on the table. We'll leave in about half an hour so we get there when the museum opens. You know how much Michael loves that place."

I do. Toothpick could look at the quirky exhibits in the Mütter Museum from open till close every day of the week if his dad would take him. I think the gross things there inspire his horror-film ideas.

"I'll be ready in a few," I say, my throat still scratchy.

After Mr. Taylor leaves, I force myself out of bed, even though I'd rather roll over and fall back to sleep until, oh, high school. The muscles in my legs are tight and sore and achy all at once. I wonder how many miles I walked yesterday. I must have set a world record or something, because it takes Mom and me three buses to get to the cemetery.

By the time I shower, brush my teeth with my finger and get dressed, my toasted bagel is hard and my eggs are cold, but they still taste good. The pink protein shake Mr. Taylor makes for Toothpick and me tastes like blueberries and bubble gum.

"Ready to go?" Mr. Taylor asks, rubbing his palms together. "We've got a birthday to celebrate. And we don't want to miss a minute of gore. Right, guys?"

"Definitely," Toothpick says, fiddling with the skinny birthday candle sticking out of a new fake neck injury. "You like my birthday wound?" he asks.

I nod, feeling like I might be sick again.

Toothpick raises a fist. "Then let the birthday festivities begin!"

His dad laughs and lends me one of Toothpick's old jackets to wear. I have to roll up the sleeves.

Toothpick nudges me and asks, "Hey, why'd you run out

of PE like that yesterday? Were you going to hurl or something?"

I nod and am grateful when Pick doesn't ask any more questions, and we get in Mr. Taylor's car to head to the museum.

Going to the Mütter Museum will be good for me, I decide. Besides the fact that we've done it almost every year on Toothpick's birthday, it will be a chance to forget everything a while longer. To put off dealing with what I'll have to face back home. And I can't even think about what going back to school Monday and facing Angus Andrews will be like.

But once we park on Twentieth Street and walk past Mama's Vegetarian Restaurant and a bunch of row houses on Chestnut Street and tromp up the stone steps to the College of Physicians, where the museum is located, and Mr. Taylor pays our admission at the front desk, I realize it was a mistake coming here.

I should have asked to go home.

My body aches. I still feel weak. And every time I think about Barkley, I feel like I'm going to puke again.

Pick runs past the giant glass display in the first room and heads down the stairs, where most of the exhibits are. I pace back and forth near the entrance, wondering how long it would take to get home if I took the El and a bus. But I don't have money for SEPTA, so it doesn't really matter. Stupid Angus has all my money.

I'm stuck here.

"Can I help you?" the lady at the front desk asks.

"No, I'm good," I say, and slink down the hall toward the first exhibit: skulls.

With my back to the exhibit, I look over the railing at the floors of exhibits below, but it makes me dizzy. So I turn toward the giant glass display case filled with shelves of skulls. Human skulls.

Since there's nothing else to do, I examine each skull and read the little card about how each person died. Some of the skulls belonged to kids who died centuries ago. Lots of the skulls belonged to teenagers who were not much older than I am, and hardly any of the skulls belonged to old people, because years ago people didn't live nearly as long as they do now.

Of course, even now, not everyone lives as long as he should. Some people get hit by a SEPTA bus or fall off the Benjamin Franklin Bridge or get a lousy disease, like lung cancer.

With each skull and story in the display case, I envision my dad lying in that hospital bed in our living room/dining room/kitchen. The skin over his face was so tight and thin and he'd lost so much weight that I could actually make out the structure of his skull—deep eye sockets, sunken cheeks.

No one should see his dad look like that.

I hurry downstairs, to the exhibits on the lower level, wondering why this place is bothering me so much today. It never did before. Normally, when we came on Tooth-pick's birthday, I found the exhibits super cool. I loved the one about how President James Garfield didn't die from a bullet wound from his assassin's gun but from the bacteria that entered his body when doctors put their unwashed fingers into the wound to try to retrieve the bullet. The bullet probably wouldn't have killed the president, but infection, because doctors didn't know to wash their hands back then, did.

Today the exhibits don't interest me at all. They're creepy and make me sick to my stomach.

What's wrong with me?

Toothpick's opening little drawers that contain items people have swallowed and had removed from their stomachs—safety pins, buttons, coins, a spoon—and he looks really excited, like I used to when we came here. I mean, there aren't too many places you can see a gigantic colon or the skeletons of a dwarf and a giant. The Mütter Museum is usually amazing.

I swallow hard a few times to calm my stomach and find one of my favorite exhibits, sure I'll feel better soon and will be able to enjoy the rest of Toothpick's birthday.

Three jars perch on a shelf in a glass case. Each jar contains a different animal brain suspended in a clear, thick liquid, probably formaldehyde. I examine the little pinkish-gray brains. The biggest of the three brains is the dog's, then a smaller cat's brain and a tiny mouse brain.

I wonder how big Barkley's brain is.

Was.

This isn't working.

I turn to another exhibit. It's a corset—some weird kind of undergarment worn by women years ago to make themselves look skinnier under their dresses. In this case, a woman had her corset tied so tightly that it pushed one of her ribs into her lung, which killed her.

Killed! By a piece of underwear!

I press my palm against my chest and feel it rise with each breath.

Dad's lungs were in bad shape. His left one was full of tumors. One time it collapsed, which must have been horrible for Dad, because after the doctors reinflated it at the hospital, I heard him tell Mom he felt like he was drowning.

Barkley basically drowned by not having enough clean water in his tank.

An ache fills my chest, then drops into my stomach. Even though I'm in an exhibit room with Toothpick, his dad and plenty of other people, I feel empty and alone.

I wonder if Barkley is still lying in that awful, toilet-paper-filled water? *Did Mom take him out and put him somewhere else? Did she—gulp!—flush him? Is Zeyde okay?*

I want to go home.

I *need* to go home.

But Toothpick is still opening the drawers of things people swallowed. And I don't want to mess up his birthday, so I walk to the next exhibit.

Why am I such a wimp?

I look at the giant colon that held over forty pounds of poop, which is kind of cool. Then the wax model of the lady with a horn on her forehead, which is neat. And President Grover Cleveland's malignant tumor. Ugh.

Dad's tumor was malignant.

Surgeons tried to cut it out—two different times—but it grew back. The stupid cancer started in his left lung and eventually spread throughout his body. I'm glad Dad's tumors aren't in this museum. They're nobody's business.

I never thought about it before, but the Mütter Museum contains collections of horrible things. I always thought they were neat, but not today. Today I feel sorry for all these people.

I feel sorry for myself.

Toothpick's standing in front of the display of the liver from the famous conjoined twins, Chang and Eng, which reminds me that he wants us to be conjoined twins for Halloween. I don't even feel like trick-or-treating this year. Pick's dumb birthday candle protrudes from his fake neck wound and quivers. He kind of looks like he could *be* in one of the exhibits.

I walk over and tug on his jacket sleeve to get his attention. "I'm going to the bathroom."

He nods, the birthday candle bobbing up and down. "You okay?" he asks. "You still don't look so good."

I don't feel so good. The contents of my stomach are roiling and making a beeline toward my throat. I'm afraid to open my mouth, so I barely nod and dart up the stairs, past groups of people walking down, past the display of skulls and past the admission desk.

I turn down a hall and hope I make it to the bathroom in time.

I do.

A stream of vomit erupts into a toilet in the first stall. I'm glad no one else is in the bathroom, because I'm making retching noises. They'd make a good sound effect in one of Pick's horror films. Bits of egg and bagel are pink from the protein shake Mr. Taylor made.

I wish Mom were here. But she wouldn't be in the men's bathroom with me even if she were, so I wish I were home. Home in bed, with Barkley swimming beside me. And Zeyde, healthy and still living with Bubbe Mary. And Dad . . . I wish Dad were still alive, sitting in his recliner in our living room/dining room/kitchen, screaming at the Eagles' head coach about a rotten play he just called.

How come I didn't realize how good I had everything back then?

After catching my breath, I go out to the row of sinks and rinse my mouth with water, but it still tastes acidy, and the back of my throat burns.

The bathroom door opens.

I'm relieved when Mr. Taylor walks in, but the look of concern in his eyes makes me feel like crying.

"Michael told me you came in here. Said you didn't look so good." Mr. Taylor presses the back of his hand to my forehead. "Hmm. Still a little warm. You feeling okay, Ben?"

This time I tell the truth without any words: I shake my head no.

He grabs me and holds me to him just as a waterfall erupts from my eyes. *What's my problem? Maybe when Angus smashed my head into the locker, he broke something in there that made me even more of a wuss.* After yesterday's waterfall, I didn't think I had any tears left inside, but apparently I do, because I blubber onto the front of Mr. Taylor's shirt like a baby.

Even though I'm soaking his shirt, he keeps holding me. When I start shivering, he holds me tighter.

"I think we'd better get you home, Ben."

I nod, even though I don't want to ruin Toothpick's birthday.

Mr. Taylor holds me even tighter. I can hardly breathe, and I don't care. It feels good. I don't want him to ever let me go.

"It's okay," he murmurs.

I know it's not, but his words feel good. His strong arms around me feel good. *It's okay*, I lie to myself. *It's okay.*

I'm glad no one comes into the bathroom, because I'm shaking and crying and snot is dripping out of my nose, and I don't even have a lousy piece of toilet paper with me to wipe it.

"It's okay," Mr. Taylor says again, his warm arms still around me. His voice reminds me of someone. "It's okay. Shh. It's okay," he keeps saying in that familiar voice as he rocks me back and forth. "It's okay, son."

I know that voice. It makes me relax a little and I whisper/cry the name of the person it belongs to: "Dad?"

Mr. Taylor pauses for a second, but then goes back to rocking me.

He hands me a couple paper towels to wipe my face, and we leave the bathroom just as two little kids barrel in, followed closely by their dad. *Lucky kids.*

I keep my head down so they can't see how not okay I am.

Toothpick's dad steers me to the tiny gift shop near the admission desk. "Wait in here, Ben. I'll get Michael."

I nod, glad the shop is empty, except for a lady working behind the counter.

I slink to the far corner of the small shop, near a rack of postcards, and keep my head down. I think the postcards would be good for my sweepstakes entries, because they have photos of the displays in the museum. They would definitely attract a judge's attention, but I don't have money to buy any, and I don't care about sweepstakes anymore.

What have sweepstakes ever given me for all my years of hard work, other than some lousy plain oatmeal packets and a bunch of useless junk in my closet? Maybe I'll never enter another sweepstakes or contest again. *Why should I waste my time?*

"Here you go, young man."

I pretend I'm studying postcards and don't hear the lady behind the counter.

She raises her voice. "Young man, you might like this contest."

I glance up, hoping my hair hides my face, which I'm sure is red and blotchy from crying in the bathroom.

She holds a sheet of paper toward me. "It's a costume contest," she says. "First year the museum's trying it. Should be fun."

Did she read my mind? *No more contests, lady behind the counter!*

Since I can't figure out how to get out of it, I walk over and take the paper from her. I mumble, "Thanks," then wait outside the entrance of the gift shop so I won't have to talk to her anymore.

I shove the paper into the pocket of Toothpick's jacket without looking at it and hope Pick and Mr. Taylor get here before anyone else talks to me.

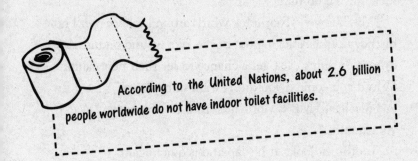
According to the United Nations, about 2.6 billion people worldwide do not have indoor toilet facilities.

Toothpick and I sit on opposite ends of the backseat of Mr. Taylor's car, and we're already passing the Mr. Barstool store on Race Street and pulling onto Interstate 95 when I realize we haven't said a single word to each other since I told him I was going to the bathroom back at the museum.

I come up with one word that might break through the invisible wall that's formed between us: "Sorry."

Looking out his window, Toothpick shrugs, like it doesn't matter.

But I can tell he's pissed that I ruined his birthday by making him leave his favorite place way before he was ready. "I'll make it up to you," I say, even though I have no idea how I'd do that.

"You know—" Toothpick whirls around to face me. The birthday candle sticking out of the fake wound on his neck droops. "I didn't even get a chance to see their new exhibit! Why'd you come if you didn't want to be there?"

"Michael!" Mr. Taylor barks from the front seat. "Watch your mouth!"

Toothpick looks at his lap and is quiet again.

I stare out the window at white-gray clouds of pollution billowing from the smokestacks of a chemical plant. Even though the car windows are closed, the stink seeps in, and I feel like I'm going to be sick again. I put my forehead against the cool window and wish I were home in bed, where I couldn't mess anything else up for anyone.

After we pass a few exits and about a billion billboards advertising WaWa and Dunkin' Donuts and Toothpick *still* hasn't said another word to me, I pull the stupid paper from the jacket pocket and look at it, because there's nothing else to do. "Pick?" I say softly.

He's silent.

"Pick?" I say a little louder, thinking he didn't hear me the first time.

"What?" he snaps.

He heard me the first time. My heart sinks a little, but I'm glad his dad doesn't yell at him again.

I pass the paper to him, like an apology.

His lips move as he reads it. "So?" he says.

I point to the grand prize money—fifteen hundred dollars—and raise my eyebrows. "We should do this."

Toothpick stares at the paper, then a tiny half smile forms. "We should," he says, excitement creeping into his voice. "I could do the makeup."

"Yes," I say, because that's exactly what I was thinking. "And I could . . . I could . . . make an, um . . . I could make a toilet paper wedding dress for the costume. That way, I could use it again for the Cheap Chic Toilet Paper Wedding Dress Contest in the summer. How cool would that be?"

In the rearview mirror, I catch Mr. Taylor grinning.

"Can you actually do that?" Pick asks. "I mean, will it hold up for the judging and all? Not fall apart?"

I think of the videos of toilet paper wedding dresses other people made. I think of the free rolls of Royal-T I've been saving in my closet. For a toilet paper emergency. "Yes," I say. "I think I can." I look across the backseat at my best friend and the droopy candle dangling from his neck. "Pick, I know I can." A part of me wishes I'd given the toilet paper to Zeyde, though, instead of saving it, because then maybe Barkley would still be alive.

Toothpick wiggles in his seat. "Okay, you'll make a toilet paper wedding dress, and I'll do the makeup. It could be a zombie-bride costume or something." Toothpick bites his lip. "Who will we get to wear the wedding gown? If you're making the dress and I'm doing the makeup, then neither of us can wear it."

I lean back. "Not that we'd want to."

"Right," Toothpick says.

We both face front.

"Don't look at me," Toothpick's dad says, glancing in the rearview mirror. "There's no way I'm wearing a toilet paper wedding dress. I've got a reputation to uphold." He laughs. "What the heck are you guys talking about anyway?"

"A contest," I say.

"Costume contest at the Mütter Museum," Toothpick adds.

"In two weeks," I say. "On a Saturday."

"Can you drive us?" Toothpick asks.

"Doubt it," Mr. Taylor says. "I usually work Saturdays. You know I asked for today off because of your birthday."

"Yeah." Toothpick sounds disappointed. "I know."

Something unpleasant settles in my gut. I turn to Toothpick and mouth the words "I'm really sorry," because I not only ruined Toothpick's favorite thing to do on his birthday, I wasted Mr. Taylor's day off, too.

Pick mouths the words "Don't worry about it." And we bump fists.

That's when I know it really is okay between us again, and I feel much better. I'm sorry I messed up his birthday, but I'm glad we're still friends. Even if Toothpick is a weirdo who sticks birthday candles, nails and broken pencils in fake wounds on his body, I'm glad I didn't lose his friendship. Because right now, I couldn't stand to lose another thing.

I lean back in my seat and tap the paper. "We're totally going to win."

"You know it," he says, plucking the candle out of his fake neck wound. "It's going to be an epic costume. Extra epic!"

"Extremely excellently extra epic!" I shout, thinking that all that alliteration would be great for a sweepstakes entry. That's when I know I could never give up sweeping. It's too much fun to think about all the great prizes I could win, even if I don't end up winning them.

Toothpick and I crack up. Even Mr. Taylor laughs. Probably at us, though.

And even though we're almost at my apartment, and I'll have a lot to deal with when I get there, I feel better than I have in a while. I'm not hot, dizzy and nauseated anymore. And I feel like something returned that's been missing— some small thing that makes a huge difference.

Hope.

COLOSSAL COSTUME CONTEST

WHERE: MÜTTER MUSEUM OF THE
COLLEGE OF PHYSICIANS
OF PHILADELPHIA,
19 SOUTH 22ND STREET

WHEN: SATURDAY, OCTOBER 31, NOON

WHAT: MAKE AND MODEL YOUR
        SCARIEST, MOST CREATIVE
        COSTUME

WHY: $1,500 GRAND PRIZE
        $500 FIRST PRIZE
        $250 SECOND PRIZE
        $100 THIRD PRIZE

In 2013, after the Super Bowl, toilet use spiked 13% in New York City. This caused a 2-inch drop in a 30-foot water reservoir in Yonkers, New York.

I feel pretty good, that is, until Mr. Taylor honks twice, Toothpick waves wildly from the front seat and they pull away. I left Pick's jacket in the car, so I shiver when a cold breeze smacks against my back.

As they drive away, my hope races off with them. A thousand people will probably enter that costume contest. There's no way Toothpick and I will win, especially not the grand prize.

I'll probably never win a grand prize.

And we'll be kicked out of our apartment after Mom's court date, which is just over two weeks away. Not to mention that on November 1, we'll owe twelve hundred dollars more. But Mom said our lease gives us a five-day grace period to pay that. *As if that will even help!*

Standing inside our apartment building, leaning against the row of mailboxes, I feel so alone. Able to glimpse the orange eviction notice on our door. Alone. Imagining waking somewhere else, without Dad's galaxy overhead. Alone.

Without Barkley.

Alone.

I need a hug from Mom. Right now.

As I take the steps two at a time and stick my key in the lock, I hope she's home. "Mom!" I yell. "Hey, Mom?"

There are a bunch of papers spread on the table, and my sweepstakes supplies are pushed to the side.

No one's in the bathroom.

I knock and go into Mom's bedroom. Her bed's neatly made, and a thick study guide lies on the foot of her bed. *Where could she be?* I glimpse Dad's he-man photo on the table beside Mom's bed, back out of her room and close the door.

I take a deep breath before opening my bedroom door, not sure I'm ready for what I'll find inside.

On the daybed, Zeyde's lying on his back with his hands folded across his chest. I close my eyelids for a couple seconds, because I can't stand seeing him positioned like that. That's how Dad looked in his coffin, hands folded across his chest. But Zeyde's snoring softly, so I know he's okay—just taking a nap.

I allow my neck to swivel slightly, and I push my glasses

up on my nose so I can see the desk and what's on top of it. Or what's not.

Barkley's tank is still there, but it's empty—completely cleaned out—no gravel, no castle, no bits of lousy toilet paper.

No Barkley.

I swallow past the boulder in my throat.

Where's Mom?

Zeyde's snores increase in intensity, and I can't believe I thought I missed that sound when I was sleeping at Toothpick's last night.

I look at the ceiling stars. They seem dimmer.

A loud snore startles me, and I know what I have to do.

I take a shaky breath, go into the living room/dining room/kitchen, grab a butter knife from the drawer and drag a chair into the bedroom. My legs are still stiff and achy, I guess from all the walking I did yesterday, so I climb onto the chair carefully and steady myself before looking up. I'm glad our bedroom ceilings are low enough for me to reach.

Zeyde snores so loudly, I hope I don't get rattled and fall off the chair.

Before I change my mind, I dig the butter knife under the first plastic star. It falls off and lands on the floor. I slip the small knife under the next star and jimmy that one off, too. Plunk. And another one and then another. Plunk. Plunk.

Soon plastic stars litter my bed and floor, and I've gotten into a determined rhythm. Reaching up to pry off the last little star, I hear, "Benjamin, what are you doing?"

I whirl around and nearly topple off the chair.

Mom's looking up at me from the doorway, her curly hair a frizzed-out mess, arms outstretched and palms up, like she's handing me an invisible box of Kirk's pizza. "What on earth are you doing? And why aren't you at the Mütter Museum with Michael and his dad?"

I pull my scrawny shoulders back and say, "If we're leaving here, these stars are coming with me." I look at the rest of Dad's galaxy—the part he painted, the part that matters—and my heart hurts because I can't use a butter knife to take that with us.

"Oh, sweetie."

I hop off the chair, drop the butter knife on my bed and put my arms around Mom. She feels so thin. "Mom—"

"Shhh," she says, and holds me, just like Mr. Taylor did. Then Mom takes my hand and leads me out of the room. "Let's let your *zeyde* sleep. He was up late last night. He felt bad about what he did and was worried about you." She touches the tip of my nose. "I was worried, too."

"I'm sorry," I say, for what feels like the zillionth time. "We left the museum because I didn't feel well."

Mom presses a hand to my forehead as we walk. "You're not warm. Feeling okay now?"

"I guess so."

"Good." Mom leads me to the table in the living room/dining room/kitchen. "Sit," she says.

I sit.

"Benjamin, I know you're feeling lousy about having to

leave here. I feel the same way." I catch Mom looking at Dad's football recliner. "Believe me."

I think of the costume contest at the Mütter Museum in two weeks, of the fifteen-hundred-dollar grand prize. I know there's probably no chance we'll win, but I say, "There's a small chance that—"

"I'm not done."

I press my lips together.

"But you can't do something stupid like leave school. Not ever. Do you hear me?"

How could I not hear her? She's sitting right across from me and raising her voice.

"I'm sorry," I say again. I'd almost forgotten about ditching. With all that's happened, it feels like such a long time ago. The thought of facing Angus at school Monday makes my stomach twist.

"The counselor called and said you skipped your afternoon classes Friday."

"I did, but—"

"Stop."

I'm glad Mom stops me from talking, because I don't want to tell her why I skipped. I don't want to tell her about Angus hurting me and stealing our rent money. Or that I walked about a million miles to Dad's grave.

"Your dad would never have wanted you to do something like that, and I certainly don't." Mom grabs my chin. "You need to promise it will never happen again."

I pull my chin from her grip. "It won't."

"Good," she says, sitting back, "because I was scared to death when I got that phone call. Until I saw you were okay, I thought I'd lost . . ."

Mom doesn't finish her sentence, but I can guess what she thought. And even though I should, I can't bring myself to apologize again, so I lower my head and feel rotten about worrying her.

She touches my cheek. "And I'm so sorry about Barkley, sweetheart. I know he meant the world to you." Mom shakes her head. "Boy, you had a rough day yesterday."

I nod, because I did have a rough day yesterday—worse than Mom will ever know—and if I try to say anything right now, a few tears might leak out.

"That's why I need to fill out these forms." Mom fiddles with the papers spread on the table. "Mrs. Schneckle brought them over. God bless that woman. We're going to put your *zeyde* in a memory-care program during the day, you know, while we're out of the apartment."

"A what?"

Mom smiles. "It's a good program, where Mrs. Schneckle volunteers. They have breakfast and lunch and entertainment, like people who play music and sing the old songs Zeyde enjoys. And the people in the program play card games. I think Zeyde will love it."

"It sounds good, I guess."

Mom bites her bottom lip. "And if he gets worse, like where he couldn't safely stay with us anymore at all, then he'll go back down to Aunt Abby's. She found a great place for him there—Cozy Corners Assisted Living and Memory Care Facility."

"He'd live at Cozy Corners?" I ask, thinking about the nice use of alliteration. "Away from everyone?"

"Away from Aunt Abby's fourteen cats." Mom winks. "She has only six, by the way. I asked."

"*Only* six?"

"Yup. The other eight are outdoor cats that she feeds sometimes."

"And by 'sometimes' you mean like twice a day?"

"Yeah, probably, knowing your aunt Abby." Mom smiles, then hands me her key. "Hey, go get the mail. I don't think we've gotten it for days. Just think of all the bills we might have missed."

When I touch Dad's nameplate, open our mailbox and pull out the envelopes, Mom's right. There are a couple bills, but there's something else among the bills.

And I can't believe it.

My hands tremble as I slide my finger under the envelope's flap.

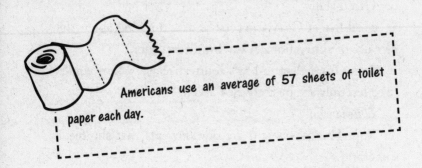

Americans use an average of 57 sheets of toilet paper each day.

I touch Dad's name on the mailbox—TODD EPSTEIN—and whisper, "Thanks."

Then I bound into the apartment, waving the mail. "Mom!"

"Shh!" She puts a finger to her lips and points down the hall, where Zeyde's snoring like a lawn mower. "What is it?"

I slide onto my chair and show her the letter from Royal-T. "This is so great." I feel like I'm going to explode from excitement. "SO GREAT!"

"Shhh!"

"Sorry." I smooth the letter in front of her, on top of the

papers about Zeyde's memory-care program. "We won," I say softly. Then I can't hold it back. "WE WON SOMETHING BIG!"

"What?" Mom asks, her eyebrows arching as she scans the letter. "What big thing did we win? Are you sure, Ben? I don't see it in this letter."

"I don't know." I'm bouncing in my seat. "That's how these things work. I've read all about them on the sweeps message boards. These letters say you won a prize but don't specify which one. But when you get an affidavit to sign like this, it means it's a big prize. Really big!"

Mom holds the letter to her chest. "Well, what do you think we won?"

My hand trembles as I run it through my hair. "I don't remember all the prizes. I was focusing on the grand prize—ten thousand dollars."

"TEN THOUSAND DOLLARS?" Mom screams.

"Shhh." I point toward my room.

Mom's voice trembles. "Do you think we might have won ten thousand dollars, Benjamin?"

"Maybe," I say, but inside I'm thinking, *Yes, yes, YES—my first grand-prize win ever. YES!*

"Oh my . . ." Mom leans back in her chair and fans herself with the letter. "By the way, what a terrific slogan you came up with!" She flicks the letter. "That's absolutely excellent."

"Thanks, Mom." I feel my cheeks heat up from the

compliment. "I couldn't have done it without Zeyde, using the word 'throne' for toilet. That's what gave my slogan that extra zing thing."

Mom smiles, and I grab my sweepstakes supplies to rummage through and see if I can find the letter with the contest information, listing all the prizes, but I have a ton of old newsletters and junk in the box and can't find it. "I might have thrown it out."

"That's okay," Mom says, catching her breath. "It will be a really nice surprise when it arrives."

"Mom, we've got to get this affidavit signed and back to them right away."

"Where do I sign?" Mom asks.

I point to the line for her signature.

While Mom signs, I ask, "Could you please send this out certified mail tomorrow?"

"I can't do that."

"Why not?" I screech, panicked.

"Because tomorrow's Sunday, Ben. The post office is closed."

"But it says we have to get this back to them within seven days or we forfeit the prize. And it's probably been sitting in our mailbox a couple days already."

"Let's mail it today. I think the post office on Rising Sun Avenue will still be open."

"Yes!"

"Let me grab my purse."

I pace the room, rereading the letter.

"By the way," Mom says, putting the letter into the return envelope. "I took my test this morning."

"What?" *That's why she wasn't home today. How could I forget? It's the most important part of the Grand Plan!*

"I was at the Prometric Test Center at 601 Walnut Street. And you know what?"

"What?"

"I think I did great. All that studying seemed to pay off."

I give Mom a fist bump. "Best day ever!"

Now I *know* Dad had something to do with making this happen. He's making sure we follow the Grand Plan even though he's not here anymore. Mom took three tests before Dad died, and somehow he made sure she took the fourth and final test, despite all the problems we're having. Even though it must have been so hard for Mom to get back on track and take that last test after losing Dad. She was so sad for so many months, she could barely do anything.

"Mom, do you think Dad has something to do with all this?"

She lets out a breath. "Benjamin, I think ... we're finally getting our footing back. At least, I am. And it's a good feeling, let me tell you. It's been like wading through a thick fog since your dad died."

The word "died" jabs at my heart. "I know what you mean." I think of my visit to the cemetery, to Dad's grave. "It's been really hard. But we're finally doing better. Right? Finally following Dad's Grand Plan, just like he wanted."

Mom nods.

"Hey, Mom, guess what."

"What?"

"WE MIGHT HAVE WON TEN THOUSAND DOLLARS!"

"Shhh!"

From a few feet away, I hear, "What are we shushing?"

I jump.

Zeyde stands there in pajamas and slippers.

"Dad," Mom says, patting her heart. "Didn't hear you come in."

"I'm sneaky like that," he says. Then he pulls up the collar on his pajama top and says, "Frankly, Shelley, I'm a pretty amazing guy."

I laugh, glad Zeyde sounds good today.

"You know who else is a pretty amazing guy?" Mom asks, grabbing me to her. "Your grandson." She gives me a noogie. "He might have won us some big money."

"Mazel tov," Zeyde says, wrapping an arm around my shoulders and pulling me in tightly.

"Yup," I say. "Maybe ten grand."

"Whoa!" Zeyde leans back. "Do you know what that would mean?"

"What?" Mom asks, now standing by the door.

"It means we can finally buy some good toilet paper."

And we all crack up.

But then Zeyde kneels in front of me, and I can tell it hurts him to bend like that, because he groans a little.

"Boychik," he says, grabbing my hand with his soft, veiny one. "I'm sorry about what I did to your fish."

I think that if I'd given Zeyde more of the good toilet paper from my closet in the first place, it wouldn't have happened.

I think about how Toothpick forgave me for ruining his birthday today.

I remember how Mr. Taylor made me feel better when I was bawling like a baby in the museum's bathroom.

I help Zeyde up, wrap my arms around him and say, "It's okay." I pat his back. "It's okay, Zeyde."

And this time, the words don't feel like a lie.

Congratulations, Shelley B. Epstein!

You've won a prize in the Royal-T Slogan Contest for your entry:
EVERY TIME YOU'RE ON THE THRONE, PAMPER YOUR POSTERIOR WITH ROYAL-T BATHROOM TISSUE!
   Please sign and return the enclosed affidavit within seven days so your prize can be delivered.

Best regards,
Royal-T Team Members

The first recorded use of toilet paper occurred in China around A.D. 851. Later, during the Ming dynasty (1368-1644), sheets of toilet paper were made from soft fabric, cut into rectangles that were two feet by three feet.

As soon as Mom and I come back from the post office, I borrow glue, tape and a needle and thread from Mrs. Schneckle, then go into my closet and pull out the ten rolls of Royal-T toilet paper I've been saving.

"Boychik, you've been holding out on me."

"Sorry, Zeyde. I was saving it for something important."

He climbs onto his bed, opens a book and leans back on a pillow. "*Nu?* I'm not important? What are they for, then? Wiping the queen's *tuchis?*"

"Gross." I show Zeyde the flyer from the museum. "I'm going to make a wedding dress out of toilet paper."

Zeyde tugs at his ear. "My hearing must be going,

because I thought you said you're making a toilet paper wedding dress."

"I am. And Toothpick's going to do the makeup to go with it."

"Somebody getting married?" Zeyde asks. "A couple of plumbers, maybe?" He laughs at his own corny joke.

I love when Zeyde's doing well, when his thoughts are clear and what he says makes sense. I wish he could be this way all the time. "It would be so cool if we could win a prize in the costume contest," I tell him. My heart speeds up, because I know I already won something big from the Royal-T contest. And I can't wait for it to be delivered, so I can find out what it is.

"A toilet paper wedding dress. That's great," Zeyde says with his words, but his face lets me know he thinks I'm crazy. "Let me know if I can help." He holds up his book. "I'll be right here reading about double-crossing secret agents and international intrigue."

"I'll let you know," I say. But this isn't something Zeyde can help with, so I get back to work.

I try weaving several sheets of Royal-T toilet paper to make a square of fabric, but it doesn't work. Then I try layering sheets on my bed, but I need something to hang the toilet paper on while I work on it. The people from one of the videos I watched had a mannequin. Maybe Mom can stand there while I make the dress on her.

I knock on her bedroom door.

"Enter if you dare."

I dare. Mom's on her bed, looking at a photo album.

"Come look," she says, patting the space beside her on the bed.

At the beginning of the album are photos of Dad and her lounging at the beach, eating cotton candy at Great Adventure, smashing cake in each other's faces at their wedding and kissing each other on their honeymoon at some hotel in the Poconos that has a champagne glass that's way taller than they are and is actually a swimming pool. I don't remember seeing this photo album before.

The next photos include me when I was a baby. In one of them, Dad holds me in one hand and a bowling ball in the other.

"When you were born, you were a big baby, but you still weighed less than Daddy's bowling ball."

"I didn't know Dad bowled."

"He was in a league—the Northeast Philly Kingpins." Mom turns the page and points to Dad standing with a bunch of other people, wearing matching collared shirts and holding bowling balls. "There's your dad with his bowling buddies. They played every Tuesday at Cottman Lanes."

I touch the picture. "His bowling shoes look ridiculous."

Mom laughs. "I always threatened to throw away those ugly things when he wasn't looking." Mom pushes the hair off my forehead. "But don't you know, they're still in my closet."

"How come I don't remember Dad bowling?"

"He started working more." Mom shrugs. "And bowling less. Gave up his bowling league a long time ago. But don't you remember that bowling party we had for your eighth birthday? It was really fun. Your dad wore his ridiculous bowling shoes that day."

"I kind of remember," I say. "Wasn't there a giant inflatable bowling pin that everyone signed?"

"Yes," Mom says. "The bowling alley gave that to you. All your friends autographed it. I don't know where that thing got to."

"We should go bowling sometime," I say.

"We should," Mom says. "You could bring Toothpick."

"And I could wear Dad's old shoes."

We look at each other and shake our heads at the same time.

Mom closes the photo album and lets out a breath. "You know, it feels good to be done with that accounting test, but a little sad. I used to spend almost every spare minute studying. And now . . ." She shakes her head. "I know it's dumb, but I feel a little lost now that it's over."

I nudge her with my shoulder.

"Hey, at least by the end of the month, we'll find out if I passed, then I'll get a good job. With benefits and everything. Won't that be great, Ben?"

"So great. Mom?" I want to tell her what happened with Angus in the locker room. I want to tell her about the rent money that got stolen. I want to tell her everything that happened yesterday, like me walking a million miles to the cemetery by myself. But that's not what comes out of my mouth. "What happened to Barkley? I mean, I know what happened, but . . . what did you do with him?"

Mom touches her head to mine. "I placed him in an empty pancake box, said a little prayer and buried him under that little patch of grass behind our apartment building. You mad?"

I take a breath and think about what she just told me. "You said a prayer for him?"

Mom nods.

"That's good. A prayer is nice."

"Mmm-hmm."

"A pancake box? Really?"

She shrugs. "It's all I had handy."

"Mom?

"Yes, sweetheart?"

"Do you think you'd be able to stand still for a few hours while I make a toilet paper dress on you?"

"Well, it's not every day someone asks me that!"

"I don't know why not."

"Hmm. While I don't have to study anymore, I do have to finish filling out those papers and get them to Mrs. Schneckle so we can get Zeyde in that program. Exactly how long would it take?"

I think about crafting an entire dress from toilet paper. "Pretty long," I say.

"Maybe there's someone else you can ask or . . . does it have to be a person?"

"What?"

Mom goes in her closet, which extends back pretty far. She pulls out a bunch of stuff, then drags out a man's body.

"What the—?"

Not a body exactly. Just the top half. A man's torso on a pole with a wide base. And the half-body is all beige.

Mom sets it upright and punches the fake man right in the face.

"Mom!"

She cracks up. "Want to punch it? It was your dad's."

"Why did Dad have half a man? With no arms? And six-pack abs?"

"Sparring practice," she says. "It's a punching dummy. Your dad got into sparring, oh, about eight or nine years ago, but when he got punched really hard in the nose once at the gym, the punching dummy went into the closet and his sparring hobby went by the wayside." She jams her fist into its face again so hard the strange half-man leans backward. "Ooh, that feels good," Mom says. "I should do this more often."

"You're weird." I get up to examine the punching dummy and wonder what other interesting Dad things Mom might have hidden in her closet. I love discovering things I didn't know about Dad. "Thanks," I say. "This might work."

I drag the half-man thing into my bedroom.

Zeyde lowers his book. "Aaah! You trying to give me a heart attack? What is that thing?"

"My dress model," I say, laughing. "Actually, it's Dad's old punching dummy."

Zeyde shakes his head. "You're meshugge!" And he goes back to reading.

I return to crafting toilet paper into something that might resemble a wearable wedding dress.

While I braid toilet paper strands, I know Zeyde's right. I am meshugge! I've got to be the only seventh-grade guy in the universe making a toilet paper wedding dress on a fake half-man with no arms.

I drop the toilet paper roll on my bed and ball my right fist. Then I stand on my toes and punch the fake man square in the nose. His head jerks back. It reminds me of the tender lump on the back of my head where Angus slammed it into the lock. I press the sore place and wince. I'm glad the scratch on my hand appears to be healing. *Thank goodness—no rabies!*

"Nice jab, kid."

"Thanks, Zeyde."

I reel back and punch the dummy again. And again. I imagine it's Angus Andrews and punch it so hard my hand hurts. *Take that, Angus.* "Wham!" A right hook hard to the cheek. "Pow!" A hard jab to the mouth. "Blam!" A powerhouse punch to the nose. "Hiyah!"

Mom's right. Punching this thing does feel good!

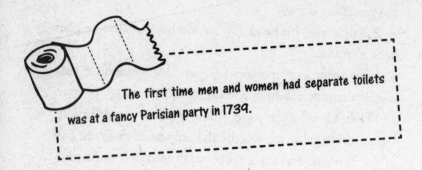

The first time men and women had separate toilets was at a fancy Parisian party in 1739.

Toothpick comes over to the apartment Sunday. I hate that he sees the orange eviction notice on our door, but he doesn't say anything about it when he comes in. And neither do I.

In my bedroom, Pick shows me magazine photos of what he wants to do with the makeup. Brains. Blood. Gore.

"It's going to be amazing," Pick says. "I'll use some of the same techniques for our Halloween costumes."

"Awesome," I say, trying to get myself more hyped about Halloween.

"*Nu?*" Zeyde asks from his bed.

"The costume contest," I remind him. "At the Mütter Museum. Remember? I showed you the flyer yesterday."

Zeyde puts a finger in his place in the book and tilts his head.

"Toothpick and I are going to make a zombie-bride costume." I sling my arm around Toothpick's skinny waist. "Right, buddy?"

"Absolutely," Toothpick says, slinging his arm around my waist.

"Interesting," Zeyde says, positioning the book in front of his face again. Then he lowers it. "I know I read this book before, but I don't remember it, so it's new to me."

Toothpick looks at me like Zeyde's crazy. I don't tell him that sometimes it seems like he is. I don't tell him anything about what's been going on with Zeyde, because that stuff is private family business. It's bad enough he saw the eviction notice on our door.

"Check this out," Toothpick says, shoving a picture in my face. "This is what we should do for the contest."

It looks like a girl's jaw is showing through her skin—like you can see through to the bone and muscle. "Can you do that?" I ask. "Looks complicated."

"Watch me," he says, opening his toolbox filled with makeup and supplies.

I love Toothpick's confidence.

Right now, I feel like my toilet paper dress is a disaster. It's uneven and bunching up where it's supposed to be smooth, but at least I'm finally getting it to look like an actual dress. In fact, the skirt part is almost finished. I'm going to add origami toilet paper roses to it later. "Now for the top part," I say, trying to remember what I saw in those videos, how they made the sleeves. "This is hard."

"Who's going to wear it?" Toothpick asks, pulling out a bunch of things from his toolbox of movie makeup.

"It'll have to be someone with a broad chest," I say, pointing to the punching dummy. "That leaves you out."

Toothpick throws his magazine at me, but I swat it away. "You're hilarious, Epstein."

"You know it," I say, banging a roll of toilet paper onto the side of my head. "We should think about this like any contest. To stand out, our entry should follow the directions exactly, show creativity and a touch of humor. Funny can make a difference in the judging."

"We're making a zombie bride, moron," Toothpick says, holding up a tube of "blood." "It'll be gross. It'll be gory. But how's it going to be funny?"

"I'll wear it."

We both turn to Zeyde.

He's lowered his book.

"I'll wear it," Zeyde says again, and I worry that his mind isn't working right and he doesn't know what we're actually talking about.

"That's okay, Zeyde, it's—"

"Pshaw!" he says, sitting taller. "I'm going to wear that wedding dress." He points at the half-finished dress hanging on Dad's punching dummy. "And I'll let that guy over there put all the crazy makeup on me. Then . . ." Zeyde stands and tugs on his collar. "Then it will be funny."

"That would be funny," Toothpick says. "It would be flippin' hilarious. Oh my gosh, I could paint a brain on your bald head."

I ignore Toothpick, even though that's a really good idea. "Zeyde? You'd do that for the contest? For us? It's all the way downtown, near the Franklin Institute. We'll have to take a bus and the El to get there."

"For you, boychik," Zeyde says, his eyes getting moist, "it's the least I can do after killing your fish."

Toothpick turns so he's facing the empty tank on my desk. His eyebrows arch in a silent question, but I don't say anything except "Thanks, Zeyde. That *would* be really funny."

And I give Zeyde Jake the biggest, tightest hug, trying to hang on to all the good parts of him . . . before they slip away.

British people pay twice as much as Germans and French for a four-pack of bathroom tissue, and almost three times as much as Americans.

On Monday, school stinks. (Worse than usual.)

But one really excellent thing happens, too.

Before first period is over, I get called to the counselor's office, and she asks me why I ran off Friday. I tell her I felt sick and thought I was going to vomit, which has a tiny bit of truth to it. She tells me I should have asked to go to the nurse if I felt sick. Then she lectures me for fifteen minutes, explaining how it's a safety issue if a student leaves campus and how worried they were about me.

Yeah, right. If they were worried about my safety, they should have stopped Angus from stealing my money and slamming my head into a lock on Friday. They should have expelled him a long time ago and sent him to a galaxy far,

far away, where there were no known life-forms. He'd have fit right in.

Of course I don't say anything. I just nod a lot and wait to hear what my punishment will be.

I'm shocked when there isn't one, just a warning never to do anything like that again.

In the locker room, I'm sweating, even though it's not at all warm. I try not to look at Angus while I'm dressing, but he slams his locker door, and I automatically look over.

He flashes a creepy smile and waggles a fancy phone before tossing it into his locker, turning the dial on his lock and walking away.

My gut turns to slithering snakes, because I know Angus was showing me the little toy *our* money bought for him. That moron wasted our rent money on a stupid phone.

At least he didn't hurt me again. Physically, anyway. He's probably glad I didn't tell on him. And his way of thanking me was to not smash my head into a lock again. *Mighty nice of you, moron!* Besides, I couldn't tell on Angus even if I wanted to, because I wasn't supposed to be selling candy bars in the first place.

In gym, Coach pulls me aside and reams me out in front of the entire class because I walked out Friday. He doesn't let me off with a warning. He makes me run humiliation laps around the gym—around the kids who are now staring at me—for the entire period.

Terrific.

By the eleventh lap, the muscles in my legs are on fire, but

I keep going by thinking about one thing: the ten thousand dollars I must have won from the Royal-T sweepstakes. I hope it's there when I get home, but I realize they'll need to receive the affidavit Mom signed before they send out my prize.

But maybe they'll make a mistake and send it anyway. Maybe it will be there when I get home. Maybe—

The bell rings, signaling the end of gym and the end of my ultra-humiliation laps. My legs and lungs hurt worse than the day I went all the way to the cemetery.

Coach smirks at me as I leave the gym.

Terrific!

"Sorry I didn't run with you during your humiliation laps," Toothpick says as we change. "I didn't want Coach to—"

"It doesn't matter."

Toothpick shrugs and goes to his locker.

I wasn't trying to be mean, but it really doesn't matter. It was just something I had to get through. By myself. What does matter is the prize I won from Royal-T, what it is and if it will arrive before Mom goes to court November 2.

When the final bell rings, I'm out of school like a rocket-propelled missile, heading straight for home and, I hope, my big win from Royal-T. But something outside the school's entrance makes me stop dead.

A kid is being escorted to a waiting police car by an officer. Mr. Sheffield is there, too.

I join a group of kids gathering near the car so I can see better.

An officer puts his hand on top of the kid's head and puts him into the backseat of the car and slams the door. That's when I get a good look at who it is, when I see the kid's scared face through the car window before he turns away.

"What happened?" I ask.

The girl next to me shakes her head. "I heard he got caught with a bunch of stolen stuff in his locker. Even had some kid's wallet in there."

The police car drives off, and Mr. Sheffield turns to us and says, "Show's over, everyone. Go home."

I run all the way home. And I'm absolutely ecstatic, because the person sitting in the backseat of the police car was Angus Andrews.

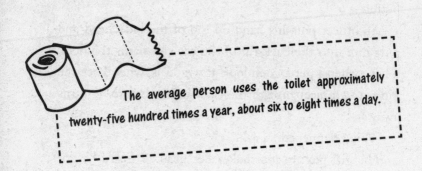

The average person uses the toilet approximately twenty-five hundred times a year, about six to eight times a day.

I yank open the door to our apartment building, step inside and stop moving. Stop breathing.

Mr. Katz stands in front of the mailboxes, talking to Mom.

"I'm really sorry, Shelley," Mr. Katz says. "I tried to talk to my partner on your behalf, but . . . my hands are tied."

Mom bites her bottom lip and nods.

Even though Mr. Katz's voice is kind, I want to sock him like I did Dad's punching dummy. It's only five hundred stupid dollars. Mom will have that much and more as soon as she passes the test and starts working at Mr. Daniels's firm. And Zeyde says he'll give us more as soon as he gets his next monthly check. *Why can't Mr. Katz's partner wait a little longer? We're almost there.*

When Mr. Katz is gone, Mom leans back against the mailboxes and exhales. "The court date is in fourteen days, Benjamin. Mr. Katz stopped by to give us one last chance to pay." Mom opens her hands. "But we just don't have it right now."

"Maybe we'll have the money by then," I say, hoping the ten grand has arrived from Royal-T already.

Mom laughs, but not a happy laugh. "I doubt it. By the time the court date rolls around, we'll owe November's rent, too—twelve hundred more. But I love that you're an optimist like your dad."

I touch Dad's nameplate on the mailboxes. "Remember the Royal-T contest?" I ask. "We definitely won something big." I reach into my pocket for the mail key and squeeze behind her. "A check might be in the mailbox right now."

I yank the little metal door open.

The mailbox is empty.

Disappointment shows on Mom's face. She trudges up the steps like each leg weighs a ton. "At least we still have two weeks left in the apartment," Mom says. "That's something."

I follow her inside. "Actually, even if things don't go well in court, we'll have at least twenty-one days after the court date before they could get the police to kick us out. I read that at the library. That's kind of good, right?"

She turns. "Yes, that's good to know, although I hope it doesn't come to that." She looks up, then at me. "By the way, I stopped by Mr. Daniels's office to make sure his offer still stood about the job."

"What did he say?"

Mom smiles. "He said as soon as I pass the test, there's a spot for me, and he can't wait for me to start."

I plop onto my chair at the table. "Looks like we're both waiting for some pretty important mail to be delivered."

"Looks like," Mom says.

For some reason, we both look at Dad's empty chair, as though it will provide some magic glimpse into the future, offer some definitive answer.

It doesn't.

Chairs are like that.

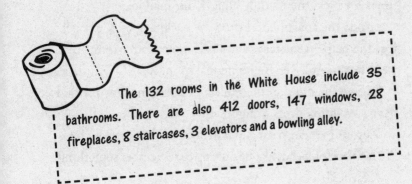

The 132 rooms in the White House include 35 bathrooms. There are also 412 doors, 147 windows, 28 fireplaces, 8 staircases, 3 elevators and a bowling alley.

Tuesday after school I stop by Toothpick's to go over some ideas for our zombie-bride costume that Zeyde will be wearing. While I'm there, I check out more videos of people making dresses out of toilet paper so I can figure out how to make the top part of the stupid dress.

The best-looking dress is one made by a bunch of art students, but they took three months to create it.

I don't have three months.

The contest is next Saturday—in only eleven days.

I tell Pick I'd better go home and work on the dress.

He's busy making his kneecap look like an exposed brain anyway, so he barely nods when I leave.

At home, even though I touch Dad's nameplate three times for luck, there's only junk in our mailbox.

Inside the apartment, I drop my backpack on the couch, toss the mail on the table and find a note from Mom: "Ben, went to the ACME. Be home real soon. XOXO Mom."

I leave the note on the table and hurry into my room. I have a wedding dress to figure out.

Zeyde's in there, pacing in the tiny space between our beds. He taps his forehead, like he's trying to remember something.

"Zeyde?"

He gasps. "You'd better hurry."

"What?" My heart races. "Hurry to what?" I wonder if something happened to Mom.

Zeyde grabs both of my shoulders. His fingers dig into my skin. "You need to tell Bubbe Mary to make her carrot *tsimmes* right now."

"Okay," I say, but it's not okay. I can't believe Zeyde seemed fine yesterday, but today . . .

"Now," Zeyde says. "Or it will never be done in time for the holiday dinner."

I used to love Bubbe Mary's carrot and raisin *tsimmes*, but that was a long time ago. I don't know how to respond to Zeyde's urgent request. "You want me to—"

"Hurry, Todd," Zeyde says, spitting on me. "Go tell Mary to make the *tsimmes*. It's Ben's favorite."

That knocks the wind out of me. He's calling me by my dad's name. "I'll tell her," I say, the words sticking in my throat. *Can't you see it's me, Zeyde?*

I run out of my room and into the bathroom, lock the door and sit on the toilet seat lid, drawing my knees in tight. *It's okay,* I tell myself. *It's okay. Zeyde will go to the memory-care program, and everything will be fine.* But I know it won't be fine, even when he goes to the program. He might be safe and have fun things to do, but it won't make him better. Mom even told me the medicine he takes only slows his memory loss but won't make him better.

Even though Zeyde is still here physically, parts of him keep slipping away.

This makes me think of Dad, of how I'm going to lose his galaxy painted on my bedroom ceiling. I think of Toothpick's mom moving far away and him seeing her only a couple times a year. And Zeyde—who's completely here one day and living in a mixed-up past the next.

And I realize there's more than one way to lose someone you love.

I tear off a stretch of lousy toilet paper and wipe my nose.

Someone knocks hard on our apartment door. As I run to answer it, I hope it's not Mr. Katz. I can't deal with him right now.

"Mrs. Schneckle," I say, grateful to see her.

"Hi, *bubeleh.*" She touches my cheek. "Your mother asked me to check on your *zeyde.* How's he doing today?"

Mrs. Schneckle must see the answer in my eyes.

"Where is he?"

I point down the hall, and she marches down there and

goes into my room. A few minutes later, Mrs. Schneckle walks out, her arm linked through Zeyde's, and she's singing some old song. Zeyde is moving his head side to side as he walks. And he's smiling.

How did she do that?

I watch them walk, arm in arm, into the living room/ dining room/kitchen.

Mrs. Schneckle helps Zeyde onto a seat at the table. "Ben," she says to me. "Do you have a deck of cards?"

I hand Mrs. Schneckle our deck of War cards, and she starts dealing and singing. Singing and dealing.

Zeyde taps the tune with his fingers on the edge of the table, then picks up his cards. "What are we playing, Celia? Five-card stud or Texas hold 'em?"

I'm stunned. He's back.

For now.

Mrs. Schneckle looks over at me and winks, so I know she has everything under control. I'm so glad that, as soon as the paperwork Mom filled out gets approved, Zeyde will go to the memory-care program at the center where Mrs. Schneckle volunteers. She'll take good care of him.

I slip into my room, take a few breaths and get to work on the wedding dress.

While I'm draping toilet paper over the punching dummy's shoulders, hoping it will fit Zeyde when I'm done, I think, *Reason #9,258 we can't lose this apartment: Mrs. Schneckle is filled with awesome!*

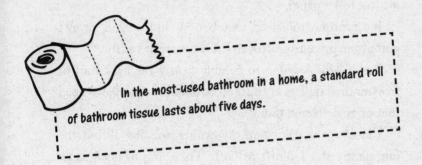

In the most-used bathroom in a home, a standard roll of bathroom tissue lasts about five days.

Zeyde seems himself on Wednesday, which is great. But the Royal-T prize doesn't arrive, which is lousy.

It doesn't come Thursday either.

And Friday is a bust, too.

After the whole next week of worrying about Zeyde, working on the wedding dress and wishing for money to miraculously appear, the Royal-T prize still doesn't arrive.

I begin to think there's been a mistake and we won't receive a prize from them at all.

I consider sending Royal-T a letter to ask about it, but I know it will never arrive in time to pay the rent before Mom has to go to court. In fact, I've been too busy lately to send them any letters at all, which means no more coupons for free toilet paper.

It's Saturday morning, October 31, and we still haven't gotten the prize from Royal-T. Of course, it's early.

But if Mom's going to be able to pay the back rent of five hundred dollars at court on Monday morning, we need that prize delivered today.

I look at the galaxy on my ceiling, missing all but the one plastic star I didn't pry off. "I'm going to need some help here," I say to the nearly starless galaxy. "Whatever you can manage would be great, Dad."

Toothpick arrives with his toolbox movie makeup kit. And I make a couple adjustments on the dress.

"It better be a heck of a good zombie, Pick. We need to win that prize money. Today." I don't tell him why, but I'm sure he can figure it out, since he saw the eviction notice on our door, which I'm sure he told his dad about. Embarrassing!

"Oh, we'll win." Toothpick looks right at me. "Wait till you see what I've been working on."

"Sounds great. And we'll split whatever we win, right?"

"Right," Toothpick says, snapping open the lid to his toolbox. "Half each. There's a summer film school I'm dying to go to, but it's really expensive. Dad said if we win that money, we'll be able to afford it."

"Awesome. Let's get to work."

I carefully remove the dress from Dad's punching dummy. By some miracle, the tape, glue and thread hold, and it doesn't fall apart instantly in my hands. I look up at the galaxy and offer Dad a silent *thank you.*

Zeyde's a real champ about me putting the dress on him. His hairy arms and legs look hilarious with the white dress.

It's just a pain when he has to pee and we have to take everything off and then put it back on.

When the dress is just right, Toothpick pulls over his toolbox and says flatly, "Leave."

"Huh?"

"Get out," he tells me. "Wait in the kitchen or something. I'll tell you when we're done. I want it to be a surprise."

Zeyde nods, letting me know he's fine with this, so I leave and go to the living room/dining room/kitchen.

Mom's there, tapping a fingernail against the table.

"What?" I ask.

"I'm restless. Let's do something."

"Sure. What?"

Mom pulls out the deck of cards, and we play about a million rounds of War until Toothpick finally calls us.

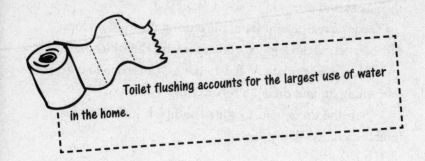

Toilet flushing accounts for the largest use of water in the home.

Toothpick skids into the living room/dining room/kitchen. He makes Mom and me stand. "Lady and, ahem, gentleman, are you prepared to feast your eyes on the toilet paper zombie bride?"

Mom smiles.

"About time," I say. "You took forever."

"All right, then," Toothpick says, ignoring my comment. He takes a deep breath and yells, "Come out, Zeyde Jake."

When Zeyde shuffles out, not only wearing the toilet paper dress but looking like he has an exposed jaw and brain, Mom screams and covers her mouth. She approaches Zeyde and examines him up close. "Unbelievable."

"Pick, it's amazing!" I punch him hard on the arm.

He rubs his arm where I punched him. "I know. Right?"

"And this dress," Mom says, touching my toilet paper creation. "It's astounding, Ben. You two are so talented."

Mom gives me a hug and kiss. And she hugs Toothpick and gives him a peck on the cheek, too.

Pick looks down, but I can tell he likes it. It's the same as how it makes me feel good when Mr. Taylor puts his hand on my shoulder, gives me a hug or tells me I did a good job at something.

"Wait a minute!" Mom darts down the hall and returns with Dad's bowling shoes. "The perfect footwear for a toilet paper wedding dress."

Mom's right. Those shoes will ramp up the funny factor.

"Ugly bowling shoes," Pick says. "Perfect, Mrs. E."

We help Zeyde put them on over his short black socks. And they fit!

Mom stands back with her hands on her hips. "Oh, *très chic*, Dad. I have to take a picture to send Abby. She'll love it!"

Zeyde strikes a pose. "Aren't I fantastic?" Then he touches the toilet paper dress, kisses his fingertips and says, "It's made from the good stuff!"

Mom gives him a kiss on the side of his face without the exposed jaw and snaps a photo with the phone Aunt Abby gave her. "You're the best!"

"I certainly am," Zeyde says. "Now, somebody help me with this thing. I need to pee again."

And we all crack up.

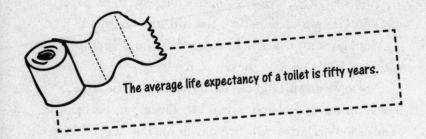

The average life expectancy of a toilet is fifty years.

On our way out of the apartment building, we see a colorful cardboard scarecrow someone taped to the door. It makes me sad that it's Halloween and Dad's not here. He loved Halloween—dressing up in crazy costumes, like the clown with the purple wig and giant sunglasses, and making a big fuss over the costumes the little neighborhood kids wore, even when they weren't that good.

Dad had a way of making people he met feel good about themselves, even little kids.

At least Toothpick and I will go trick-or-treating tonight in his neighborhood. Pick told me he has the two shirts sewn together already and will only have to do our makeup before we go out. I just hope we win something today, or my heart won't be in it.

I shake those thoughts from my head and enjoy the cool air as we walk together to the bus. We pass a couple people who do a double take, then nod their heads.

"Cool," some lady says.

Zeyde nods.

On the El, a guy asks, "Is that dress made out of toilet paper?"

When I say, "Yes," he says, "That's the best costume I've ever seen."

Zeyde, hanging on to a pole in the middle of our train, smiles at the compliment, which looks especially creepy with Toothpick's zombie makeup and Zeyde's unnaturally long ear hair.

It's a long walk from the El to the Mütter Museum, and I'm afraid Zeyde will get tired or the dress will rip, but neither of those things happens. He leaves his jacket unzipped, and lots of people stop to look at us and laugh or tell us it's a great costume.

I'm getting pumped.

We have to walk under a dingy bridge that drips water. Toothpick and I hold our arms around Zeyde to keep him and the dress dry.

I'm glad when we finally pass under the bridge and arrive at the museum.

Mom holds Zeyde's hand to help him up the steps in the dress.

The mummy manning the admission desk asks, "How many?"

My throat tightens. I didn't think about having to pay admission.

Mom puts her palm on the counter. "One adult, two students and a zombie bride, please."

I love my mom.

"The bride's free," the mummy says, smiling through her bandages. "The other three will cost a total of thirty-five dollars."

I'm sure Mom can't afford this. She's not working. How could she have any money? I feel embarrassed in front of Toothpick. And disappointed that we won't be able to get in, after all the work we did. Maybe Zeyde could go in by himself, and we could wait outside. But what if he gets confused and messes up? Or needs help with the bathroom? I wish we had thought of all wearing costumes, so we wouldn't have had to pay.

Before I can continue worrying, Mom pays for the tickets.

Go, Mom!

She leans down and whispers in my ear, "Aunt Abby sent a few bucks to tide us over."

I whisper back, "Thank you, Aunt Abby!"

"Indeed," Mom says quietly.

It's crazy crowded in the museum today, but we find the table where some guy with an arrow sticking out of his head registers us and gives Zeyde a number to wear—113—which I hope isn't unlucky.

We are stationed in the big room with most of the exhibits, where last week I told Toothpick I had to go to the bathroom and proceeded to ruin his birthday. In addition to the display cases, it's wall-to-wall werewolves, vampires, mummies, monsters and even some zombies.

But Zeyde is the only zombie bride. And definitely the only person wearing a toilet paper wedding dress. I'm really glad I thought of that.

Toothpick elbows my ribs, which reminds me of the lady whose corset was so tight it pushed one of her ribs into her lung. "I can't believe how good some of these costumes look," Pick says.

"I know." I bite a fingernail.

"I need to ask a few of them about their makeup techniques."

"Yeah," I say, distracted, as I size up the competition.

"Do you think we have a shot?" Toothpick asks. "I mean, look at that girl." He points. "Her face looks like melting lava. And that guy with the knife through his skull and the bloodied costume. It looks so real."

"I know," I say. "But I'm worried that Zeyde—"

"Shhh," Mom says, nudging me. "They're judging the costumes now."

The contestants are asked to stand around the perimeter of the room. People without costumes step far enough away that there's space for the judges to walk past each contestant. There are so many contestants, they encircle the entire room!

The rest of us are jammed together around the displays in the middle, including the corset-lady display. I'm holding Zeyde's jacket. And even though it's cold outside and usually cold in the museum, I'm sweating because of the heat generated from all these people. I hope Zeyde isn't sweating too much into the toilet paper dress. I want to use it again for the contest this summer.

Three judges holding clipboards examine each contestant and scribble notes. I try to see what they write about Zeyde, but I can't get close enough. I do manage to give Zeyde a thumbs-up. His smile looks particularly creepy with his big, fake white teeth and the jawless-zombie makeup on his cheek and chin.

After what seems like forever, the judges go back to their table and talk to one another.

We huddle near Zeyde.

"This is making me nervous," Zeyde says. "I've got to pee."

"But we don't want to miss the announcement of the winner," Mom says. "Can you hold it?"

I can't believe she asks Zeyde if he can hold it, like he's a little kid.

"Of course I can't," he says, indignant. "And I'll need one of you numbskulls to help me with this thing." He touches the sides of his dress.

"No problem," I say and maneuver Zeyde through the crowds, toward the bathrooms.

Toothpick comes, too.

Standing in front of the bathroom door, Zeyde pauses and says, "Not sure which bathroom I should use. I mean, I am wearing a dress."

We push Zeyde into the men's room and help him with the dress. Of course, he takes forever washing his hands.

"Hurry, Zeyde. We don't want to miss the big announcement."

As soon as we maneuver him back downstairs, Mom grabs my hand. "You made it just in time. They're announcing the winners now."

Mom tightens her grip on my hand. I grab Zeyde's hand. And he holds Toothpick's. We're a zombie-bride train of jangled nerves.

Please. Please, I think, hoping that somehow Dad is here with us in spirit and will help us win a prize.

Mom squeezes my hand hard when they announce the $100 third prize. It's the lady with the melting-lava face.

Toothpick looks over and mouths the words, "Told you she was good."

I nod, my stomach twisting into pretzel knots. *We have to win.*

Zeyde doesn't win the $250 second prize or the $500 first prize either.

I can't breathe.

"And our grand-prize winner is . . ."

My heart beats so hard I hear it in my ears.

The crowd falls silent.

Mom squeezes my hand so tightly, it feels like she's crushing all the bones in it, but I don't pull away.

"... that's the winner of the fifteen-hundred-dollar grand prize. And it goes to ..."—there's an unbearably long pause—"... number one thirteen—the zombie bride wearing a toilet paper wedding dress."

People cheer and pound Zeyde on the back. I notice that some of the toilet paper rips, but I can fix it later.

Other contestants lower their heads and skulk away.

Mom squeezes my neck so hard in a hug, I'm surprised it doesn't snap. "Oh my ..." Then she lets go, holds my shoulders and looks in my eyes. "You did it, Benjamin. You did it!" Then Mom looks up at the ceiling and pumps her fist. "Woohoo!"

Toothpick pulls me into a hug, slapping the back of my head. We start jumping around like idiots. My glasses bump up and down on my nose.

"We won! We won!" he screams.

Even after we let go of each other, Toothpick is still jumping. He looks like a flamingo on a pogo stick.

"We won," I say, dazed. Mom will be able to pay our back rent in court Monday. "Oh, yeah!" I pump my fist in the air, narrowly missing the nose of a vampire.

Mom puts her arm around Zeyde and leads him to the judges' table. Toothpick and I follow. People touch Zeyde's shoulder or pat his back as we pass. They say things like "Congratulations" and "Great costume, man."

It feels like they're saying "Congratulations" to me, because I finally won a grand prize.

At the table, one of the judges says, "That is the best makeup I've ever seen."

Toothpick beams.

A judge hands the check to Zeyde.

Mom gives him a huge hug and plucks it from his fingers. "This belongs to the boys." And she hands it to me. "You did it, Ben. You finally won a grand prize."

"With Toothpick's help. And yours and Zeyde's." I look up. *And Dad's.*

A reporter from the *Inquirer* asks us questions, and a photographer takes our picture. Toothpick and I hold the check in front of Zeyde, and Mom stands next to me.

"I guess you're really on a roll," the reporter says. "Get it?"

His dumb joke reminds me of Dad, and I know he'd love that we're going to be in the newspaper he used to work for.

"We'll have to send the article to Aunt Abby when it comes out," Mom says, giving my shoulders a squeeze.

"I'm going to be famous," Zeyde says.

Toothpick and I take turns holding the check and looking at it all the way out of the museum, but then we give it to Mom for safekeeping.

She puts it in her purse, then leans over and whispers in my ear, "Your dad would be so proud of you."

Her words make me happy and sad at the same time.

Zeyde zips his jacket this time. "I'm pooped!"

"Great job, Dad," Mom says. "You deserve a rest."

When we're out the door, down the steps and walking under the dank, drippy bridge toward the El, Mom says, "I'd take us all out to celebrate, but I have only enough cash left to get us home."

Knowing that Mom has a check for fifteen hundred dollars in her purse, this makes us crack up.

Actor Dick Wilson, who portrayed Mr. Whipple on TV's Charmin bathroom tissue commercials, landed in the *Guinness Book of World Records* for the longest-running TV character, with 504 ads. Procter & Gamble sent the actor complimentary rolls of Charmin bathroom tissue monthly.

Back at our apartment, I'm irritated that the eviction notice is still on our door. I feel like, since we have the money to pay our back rent, it shouldn't be there for everyone to see, but of course Mr. Katz doesn't know that yet.

Inside, Zeyde pats the dress and says, "I'll take this thing off as soon as I get a snack. I've got to eat before I *plotz*."

"There's cheese and crackers," Mom says. "Want me to get them?"

"I can get them," Zeyde says, and shuffles off to the kitchen.

"I'm going to head home," Toothpick says. "I've got to feed Psycho. And I can't wait to tell Dad. Now I can go to film camp this summer!" He pumps his skinny arm into the air. "It's going to be awesome!"

"I'll go to the bank Monday," Mom says, "and bring your half to you in the evening, if that's okay."

"That'll be great, Mrs. E.," Toothpick says. "See you later, Ben. Make sure you're at my place by five so we can get ready to trick-or-treat. It will take me a while to do our makeup. And I want to hit the streets by six for maximum candy collection."

"I'll be there," I say. "And hey, thanks for everything." We bump fists, then shoulders. "We wouldn't have won without your great makeup artistry."

"And your great toilet paper dress."

"I guess we make a good team, Pick."

"The best," he says.

After Toothpick leaves, I hear Zeyde open a cabinet and some drawers in the kitchen. "You think he's okay?" I ask Mom. "He must be tired."

She nods. "He'll probably take a nap. I'll check on him in a sec." Mom pulls me over to the couch. "I have something to tell you."

"First, I have something to tell you," I say. I'd been thinking about how to say it the whole way home. "I want you to keep my share of the prize—seven hundred fifty dollars—to pay at court this Monday. Or just five hundred. Take whatever you need."

Mom smiles. Her worry wrinkle is nowhere to be found. "Benjamin Epstein"—she takes my cheeks in her palms—

"do you know how much you're like your father? Hope-filled. Always finding a way."

She kisses the top of my head.

"But I want you to understand something." Mom takes my hand. "This ends here."

"What?"

"Your feeling you need to somehow support me," Mom says. "The contests, the candy bars. You don't need to take care of me anymore, honey. I'm . . . I'm okay now. I can take care of myself. And take care of you. And Zeyde. How does that sound?"

I nod, because it sounds so good that if I say anything, I might cry.

"As far as your prize money goes," Mom says, "I will use it to pay the back rent and any fees at court on Monday, but then I'm paying you back. Every dollar." She bites her bottom lip. "That's what I wanted to talk to you about."

Mom pulls an envelope from her purse.

For a second, I think it's the ten-thousand-dollar check from Royal-T.

It's not. Mom takes a letter from the envelope, unfolds it and points to the number 79. "Look, honey, I got a seventy-nine on my CPA exam."

I don't know why Mom's so excited. "Isn't seventy-nine a C?" I ask. "Not to be mean or anything, but isn't that kind of bad? I know you studied a lot and everything, but—"

Mom laughs so hard she spits on me. "Ben, on the exam, you need to earn a seventy-five to pass. The top score I could have gotten was an eighty, and I got a seventy-nine. So that's pretty terrific. Right?"

"Yeah," I say. "I guess that's like getting a high A."

"Exactly!" Mom hugs me and talks into my hair. "Mr. Daniels said I could start as soon as I passed the last CPA exam, and I passed. Now I'll have a wonderful new job."

"Yeah," I say. "One that doesn't require you to wear a stupid paper piggy hat."

"Nope," Mom says, patting her head. "I'll only need to wear my thinking cap."

We both laugh at her dumb joke.

Someone knocks at the door, and Mom startles.

"I'll get it," Zeyde offers, shuffling out of the kitchen in the wedding dress and Dad's bowling shoes. He's munching on a slice of cheese.

"That's okay," Mom says, her hand on the doorknob. "I think you'll scare whoever's on the other side, Dad."

Mom opens the door without asking who it is, and a woman in a brown uniform hands something to Mom. "Delivery from Royal-T Bathroom Tissue. Please sign here."

Mom and I look at each other.

"Can you tell us what it is?" Mom asks, her voice shaky.

"I can bring it in," the deliverywoman says.

She goes back outside.

Zeyde hikes up the wedding gown, carefully sits on a chair and kicks off the bowling shoes. "Oh boy, I'm exhausted," he says, seemingly oblivious to the major event about to take place in our apartment.

Mom and I wait by the open door, clutching each other's hands even more tightly than we did at the Mütter Museum.

The deliverywoman carries in a huge brown box and puts it near our couch.

"What on earth?" Mom asks, going over to the box.

I join her, confused. "That box is way too big to hold a check," I say. "Unless it's a giant check."

The deliverywoman leaves and comes back with another huge box, the same size as the first.

Mom grabs scissors from a kitchen drawer and opens one of the boxes.

And I can't believe what's inside.

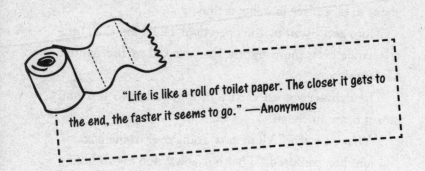

"Life is like a roll of toilet paper. The closer it gets to the end, the faster it seems to go." —Anonymous

Zeyde peers in and pulls out a roll of toilet paper. He puts it to his cheek. "Ahh, the good stuff."

When the deliverywoman comes back with a third box, Mom asks, "How many more boxes do you have?"

"Seventeen," the woman says. "Looks like you won a ten-year supply of Royal-T Bathroom Tissue. Congratulations!"

Mom and I look at each other.

I swallow hard. "A ten-year supply of—"

"Toilet paper!" Zeyde shouts, tossing a couple rolls into the air.

Mom leans her forehead against mine. "It's okay, Ben. We don't need that money."

"But—"

"We're fine," Mom says, hugging me to her. "We're going to be fine now."

And I know she's right. We have enough money to pay the back rent at court Monday and keep our apartment. Mom passed her test with an excellent score and is going to start a great new job. And Zeyde will have a safe place to go during the day, where Mrs. Schneckle can keep an eye on him. Even Toothpick gets to go to summer film camp now that we won the grand-prize check today at the museum. And we'll have enough toilet paper to last until I graduate from college . . . or medical school, if we're conservative in our usage.

I sit on top of one of the boxes and watch as the rest are delivered. They take up our entire living room/dining room/kitchen and part of the hallway.

I borrow Mom's phone to tell Toothpick about my big win. "Bring over a bunch of rolls," he suggests. "We can be mummies tonight for Halloween instead. Conjoined mummies. It'll be so cool."

When I hand Mom the phone, she shakes her head. "Benjamin, what are we going to do with all these boxes? Do you think Mrs. Schneckle would like some toilet paper?"

Zeyde and I push a whole box of toilet paper across the hall to Mrs. Schneckle's apartment.

She invites us in for a few minutes, and we tell her about winning the contest today and the special delivery we just received.

"That's wonderful," Mrs. Schneckle says, squeezing my cheeks between her warm palms. "I sure appreciate all this toilet paper. Royal-T is my favorite brand. I'll bring some to the center."

Mrs. Schneckle won't let us leave until we take a container of matzoh ball soup and a package of macaroons.

Back at our apartment, while Mom and Zeyde figure out how to stack and arrange the boxes to take up the least amount of room possible, I grab the butter knife from a kitchen drawer and scrape that stupid orange eviction notice off our door. I should have done it sooner.

There's still some white paper stuck to the door when I'm done, but we'll get it off later.

Then Mom and I help Zeyde out of the toilet paper wedding dress and hang it on Dad's punching dummy. While Mom removes the makeup from Zeyde's head and jaw with Vaseline, I do something important.

I find a tube of glue and drag a chair into my room.

There are a couple dozen plastic stars I have to put back up in their galaxy.

Toothpick and I are working on a new horror film—The Meshugge Mummies from Remington Middle.

And Mom got me a new betta fish. He's brighter blue than Barkley was and loves swimming around the plastic treasure chest Zeyde bought for him. I named him Ed.

Thanks so much for everything!

Your friend,
Benjamin Epstein

P.S. You don't have to send any more coupons for free toilet paper. ☺

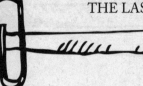

Dear Mr. Ed Chase,

Mom and I were so excited to find my slogan in a magazine while we were shopping in ACME. Mom bought five copies and cut out the Royal-T ads. She sent one to Aunt Abby in Florida, gave one to Mrs. Schneckle across the hall, handed one to Zeyde, put one up on the fridge where our Grand Plan used to hang, and we taped one on Dad's headstone.

Mom loves her new job, and she doesn't have to wear anything on her head except hair. She joked that since she works for an accounting firm, she should wear a hat that looks like a piggy . . . bank.

Zeyde is the Wii Bowling champ at the day program where Mrs. Schneckle volunteers. Sometimes he wears Dad's bowling shoes, just to crack up the other people in the program. He's pretty hilarious . . . on his good days. And I can almost tolerate his seismic snoring because of the new, industrial-strength earplugs Mom bought me.

Down in Florida, Aunt Abby has adopted two more cats— Peavy and George. Mom says we'll visit this summer, but we'll stay at a nice, cat-free hotel nearby.

GLOSSARY OF YIDDISH WORDS

boychik	young boy
bubbe	grandmother
bubeleh	darling (usually used to address children)
farkakt	crappy
latke	potato pancake, traditionally served at Chanukah
Mazel tov!	Congratulations!
mensch	honorable, decent person
meshugge	crazy
Nu?	Well? . . . So? . . . What's going on?
Oy vey!	Woe is me!
plotz	faint
shivah	Jewish mourning period of seven days, observed by family and friends of the deceased
shmendrik	nincompoop
shnoz	nose
tsimmes	dish of mixed fruit and/or vegetables
tuchis	rear end, buttocks
zeyde	grandfather

ACKNOWLEDGMENTS

It took a long time to write this book, so there are a lot of people to acknowledge. If you want to read a book with a shorter acknowledgements page, check out *Olivia Bean, Trivia Queen*. I wrote that book in twenty-nine days, and it doesn't *have* an acknowledgments page.

This book would not exist without the patient guidance from my stellar agent, Tina Wexler from ICM Partners, who took the time to help me develop not only this book, but all my published books. Vanessa, David, Olivia and now Benjamin exist because of her many talents and unwavering belief in me and my work. Thank you, Tina, for your support and behind-the-scenes help, time and again.

Sincere thanks to my editor, Michelle Poploff, who shared my enthusiasm for Benjamin Epstein's zany story and helped me tell it in the best way possible. Thanks for waiting until the story was ready, asking all the right questions and trusting that I'd come up with the answers.

Thanks to Lisa McClatchy for booking my school visits and offering wise counsel. And to her daughter, Eirann, for rocking my socks with her creative writing during a workshop at the Thurber House.

Paul Grecian shared a story that was the catalyst for this book, even though it appears nowhere in these pages. Because sometimes telling a good fictional story means letting go of the real story that inspired it. Thanks, Paul.

Nicole, I told you I'd put the Mütter Museum in my next book. Thank you for taking me there when I visited Philly. And thank you for being such a light in our lives.

For my brothers-in-law, Jay, Denny and Mike, for sharing their real-life careers with the characters in this book. With special appreciation to Mike Gephart for sending extensive information about the requirements to become a CPA in PA.

Hugs to my sister, Sherry, who has good taste in all things—especially the amazing men in her life, Ben and Ethan.

My dad, an eternal optimist and avid reader, has been my first reader and most ardent supporter. Thanks, Dad.

To my nephew Kyle, who makes sure I call a WaWa hoagie a *hoagie*. Thanks, buddy, for keeping me well grounded in my Philly roots.

My writing friends are family to me. They appear in some way on each of these pages . . . and on the pages of my heart. Love to Sylvia, Linda, Dan, Janeen, Stacie, Shutta, Diane, Gail, Laura, Ruth, Amanda, Becca, Ann, Maryann, Amy, Carole and Peter. And a special bouquet of gratitude (and cupcakes) to Jill Nadler—aka

Riley Roam of pageturneradventures.com—for checking in with me as we kept each other accountable while writing our books. Every. Single. Day.

To Jeanne, for sharing her friendship with me since we were fourteen. And for sharing her last name for this book. Steve, Jeanne, Cara, Elyssa and Jared—you Epsteins rock!

With much love to my Florida friends for keeping me connected to the "real" world with encouraging messages, long walks, kayak excursions, tea breaks, yoga classes, bike rides, embarrassing games of tennis and lots of laughter. Love you, Carilynn, Holly, Nancy, Pam, Elysa, Sharon, Sandra, Deborah, Micah, Jen, Kim, Carol, Liz, Marsha, Wendy and Cousin Jo.

Even though they can't read this, I appreciate my loyal canine companions—Teddy and Benji—for providing company while I worked and a great excuse for breaks from the computer to go on walks together. They also protected me from dangers, such as the UPS man delivering a package, the trash truck rumbling down the street and that ferocious bunny in our front yard. (Sadly, our window blinds will never be the same.)

Sending library love to local media specialists and librarians who supported me from the start: Lisa Petroccia, Carol Groceman, Debbie Remington, Helen Zientek, Sue Sloan, Amanda Bosky, Cookie Davis and

Jennifer Salas. Thanks to all media specialists and librarians for making books and reading accessible and FUN.

For the unique opportunity to spend a month in James Thurber's boyhood home in Columbus, Ohio, writing and leading writing workshops for young people, a huge thank-you to the wonderful folks at the Thurber House. And especially to Pat Shannon for taking me to some very cool places and to Meg Brown for being an awesome friend during thunderstorms, Kroger trips, a stop for sushi, late-night visits to Jeni's Ice Cream and much more. The residency lasted a month, but the memories will last a lifetime (unless I get a sharp blow to the head).

To my sons, Andrew and Jake, for putting up with me. It's not easy living with a writer who lives with a whole other family in her head much of the time. And then tells you to clean your room and turn down the music the rest of the time. Seriously, you two have enriched my life in ways I can't measure. You lovely young men are, without a doubt, my most important creative contribution to this planet.

To my endlessly interesting, always open-minded, big-hearted best friend, my husband—Dan the Man. I love our adventures together. I love YOU!

ABOUT THE AUTHOR

DONNA GEPHART spent much of her childhood at the Northeast Regional Library in Philadelphia, reading books such as *Mr. Popper's Penguins; Ben and Me: An Astonishing Life of Benjamin Franklin by His Good Mouse Amos;* and *The Hundred Dresses.* She lives in South Florida with her family, where she writes, kayaks, bikes, explores parks and beaches, and visits bookstores and libraries.

Donna's other novels are *Olivia Bean, Trivia Queen; How to Survive Middle School;* and *As If Being 12¾ Isn't Bad Enough, My Mother Is Running for President!,* which won the prestigious Sid Fleischman Humor Award. Learn more at donnagephart.com.